To Al,

All the memories.
Friendship lasts
forever and that's
true of us!

Con Amore,

Giuseppe Vincenzo Vumbuca

Praise for
The Ghost of Bowdoin College

"This is a phenomenal debut book! From the first page, all the way through till The End, the author keeps you guessing. The characters are so well-drawn they feel real. And the plot? Oh my, what a ride! I can't wait for the second book in this series."
--- D. D. Scott, Bestselling Author

It's 1805, and as a result of two tragic incidents, the legend of The Ghost of Bowdoin College is born.

Enter Vincent Mark, over a century-and-a-half later, a Bowdoin graduate and young lawyer who works for The Sterling Works in New York City. A series of suspicious deaths of senior officers at The Sterling Works, an old and unexciting New York Corporation, coupled with the launch of a sudden, mysterious, hostile takeover attempt, thrusts Mark to the forefront of defending his company, his position and ultimately his life.

Overwhelmed by the enormity of the challenge, Mark turns to his childhood friend, Anthony Vacarro, Capo of one of Brooklyn's notorious Cosa Nostra crime families. Although he has been out of touch with Vacarro for several years, trying to leave his past behind him, Mark joins with Vacarro to unravel the fast-paced developments of the hostile takeover attempt.

Throughout the wild ride, The Ghost attempts to guide Mark and another Bowdoin alumnus, Assistant Attorney General Angela Dominica.

More murders, thrilling car chases, power struggles, flashes of romance and unending intrigue thrust Mark into the fight of his life, all while he struggles to define himself.

"There are more things in heaven and earth, Horatio, Than are dreamt of in your philosophy."

William Shakespeare, *Hamlet*
Act 1, Scene V

This Book is Dedicated to Lee.
My Friend, My Lover, My Wife

THE GHOST

OF

BOWDOIN COLLEGE

Money. Murder. And the Mob.

by

Giuseppe Vincenzo Vumbacco

First Electronic Edition: August 2018

First Print Edition: August 2018

eBook and Print Book Design & Formatting by
D. D. Scott's LetLoveGlow Author Services

Table of Contents

PROLOGUE

How many of us do foolish things in our youth? Too many, far too many. But most of us, either by the benevolent hand of God, or perhaps the Boethius Wheel of Fortune, are spared the consequences of our actions. Occasionally though, our destiny is forever altered because of the unintended result of a choice we make; not well thought out, mind you, but a choice nevertheless.

Among us, too, there appears to be broad belief in angels, but what about ghosts? Can such spirits exist, and if so, why are they here? Are they serving penance for a human's foolish choices? Or do such ghosts have a mission or a purpose?

What you will encounter between these pages, may cause you to think about such things and the foolish choices you've made...

Chapter 1

The Ghost of Bowdoin College
December 7, 1805
Brunswick, Maine

Snow fell softly onto the hard Maine earth. Jonathan David Edwards carefully moved along the slippery path, taking each step with great care. No falling today. No twisted ankles. Tonight was too important!

Jonathan would soon be meeting his beloved. For the past two years, he had dreamt of this moment. He was now twenty-two years, and just a few months away from completing his studies at Bowdoin College, an all-male institution nestled in the tall pines of Brunswick, Maine.

Mary, his fiancée, was the only child of George Benjamin Howell, Professor of English Studies and Rhetoric. Professor Howell did not like Jonathan. He especially did not like to see his daughter with Jonathan, and he most certainly would never have given his permission for their marriage.

Marriage, of course, was exactly what Jonathan and Mary planned. Jonathan did not care if they received the blessing of Mary's father, her mother or anyone else for that matter. Mary loved him and trusted him with all her young heart.

Tonight, at precisely 9:00 PM, they would meet at Mere Point, where the Atlantic waters crushed against the granite rocks of the Maine seacoast. Here, they would make their final preparations.

Jonathan would complete his degree in May, and on June 1st, the two would swiftly make their journey into the City of Boston, where arrangements were nearly completed for their marriage, with the ceremony to be performed by Jonathan's older cousin, a newly-ordained congregational pastor.

Jonathan was enormously confident of all the details. He had planned this for months.

With her young heart beating rapidly, Mary silently slipped from her upstairs room and out the back door. Off she scurried, shrouded in her black cape – a solitary figure racing to her destiny.

Just as Jonathan reached their secret meeting place at the Point, he spied a raven. Odd to see a raven at this hour, he thought, especially in the snowfall. He was reminded instantly of the ancient symbolism of ravens – bad luck. But how utterly absurd. This wasn't a cheap Gothic novel. The raven eyed him curiously, and then ever so slowly, it moved its large, black wings and lifted up over the bone-chilling waters, disappearing into the darkness.

At just that moment, Jonathan heard Mary's approach.

"Oh, Jonathan, I could barely tolerate our hours apart," she gushed in a sweet whisper. "Mother kept asking me why I'd been so excited today."

She rushed forward to embrace her love with the innocent, pure enthusiasm of the very young. At that instant, however, her foot slipped, as so many things in life do, and she fell into the icy, dark Atlantic waters, hitting her head on the granite rocks. In just those few seconds, she disappeared...forever.

Jonathan stared in horror. This couldn't be happening. It wasn't real. His brain processed the information, but he could not move his body. Finally, after agonizing seconds, he lunged forward, jumping into the frigid waters.

Frantically, he thrashed about in the sea, clinging to the boulders so he would not be swept away, but there was no sign of his love. No Mary. She was gone – forever lost to him.

The days that followed were dreamlike, filled with desperation for answers that simply didn't exist. The search ultimately recovered Mary's body. But the funeral and formal inquest were a blur. There was no finding of criminal action on the part of Jonathan, but the shock, despair and pain were overwhelming.

Of course, he could not focus on his studies or anything else for that matter; nor could his parents or pastor cousin drag him away from the Bowdoin campus.

Two weeks after the horrid event, on a dark Monday morning, the aging, crippled custodian of Winthrop dormitory made his morning rounds and entered Jonathan's room – #208 Winthrop.

As he opened the door, the sight, from which he never fully recovered, shocked the poor man horribly.

Hanging from the ceiling was Jonathan David Edwards, and he was quite dead. A black raven was perched outside the window, its eyes fixed on the chilling scene. It was, indeed, a Gothic spectacle, cheap or otherwise.

Chapter 2

1806
Bowdoin College, Brunswick, Maine

Exactly one dreadful year had passed since the tragic drowning of Mary Howell and the gruesome suicide of Jonathan Edwards. However, as it is with human nature, memories fade quickly. With the sorrowful departure of Professor Howell and his wife, the campus wounds inflicted by the two deaths healed-over. Bowdoin had a new Dean and a new Freshman Class. The brilliant splendor of Fall had faded into the frigid white blanket of Winter's snow. Students prepared their lessons, and professors instructed them with vigor.

One Friday evening, three Bowdoin students in their third year had completed their noisy, rather sloppy, consumption of thirteen pints of Maine's finest lager. They were gloriously drunk.

Alcohol in general, and beer in particular, has a rather unique way of ratcheting up testosterone in who might otherwise pass for ordinary men with ordinary sensibilities. With the appropriate injection of grain alcohol, the meekest creatures can be transformed into raging bulls. These three had arrived at that splendid point of inebriation where they could perfectly perform the most stupid acts imaginable. Such was the case that very evening.

Since the hanging the previous year, Bowdoin's President had ordered Room 208 in Winthrop Hall to be locked and barred to all students. And so, it remained...until that night.

The trio decided it was high time to breach the barrier to mysterious Room 208 and find out what was really behind the door.

"Listen carefully, men," grunted Trevor, leader of the beer brigade. "We're all agreed that in thirty minutes, at precisely 11:00 PM, we will meet at Winthrop Hall, second floor. Thomas, you will bring the carpenter's small stoop bench. Winston, you will fetch a common broad hammer and wedge. I, of course, will bring the lantern. The night watchman concludes his walk along the path to Massachusetts Hall at precisely 10:15; he then passes through the ground floor of Winthrop, exiting the other side on his way to the west end of campus. By 11:00 PM, we can safely carry out our mission."

Between belches, the three embraced then slithered...or staggered...depending on your perspective, off their separate ways. Surprisingly, considering their level of inebriation, Trevor, Thomas and Winston all reassembled with their tools at more or less 11:00 PM.

Trevor held the lantern high while Thomas stood on the bench and jammed the wedge against the door. He started hammering. The heavy oak door groaned, and with several more loud and aggressive raps, it began to splinter. As the door handle flew off, they all roared with drunken approval.

Winston pushed Thomas aside and grunted, "Stand aside, mate, while a real man plies his trade."

With great force, he jammed the wedge between the door edge and the molding and then threw his entire weight against the lever. The door creaked but held. Thomas added his body to the next thrust, and the two cursed heartily as they gave their all.

The molding cracked, the door flew open and the three grinned devilishly as they stumbled into the room.

Trevor passed his lantern slowly from left to right. The room appeared empty and heavy with dust.

"There's nothing here!" He screeched. "It's barren! Not a stitch of furniture. No chair. No noose. It's void! I wonder if there really was a hanging here."

Given the commotion, several of the Winthrop residents had left their rooms and crowded around the entrance. None, however, entered.

Trevor farted, followed by a belch and then spat upon the floor. "Bloody Administrators, for some reason, they've concocted a lie. They didn't want us in here, but it isn't because of any hanging."

At precisely that moment, a white specter arose from the floor, ever so slowly at first, then with more speed and definition. It took on the rough appearance of a human, only this was no human, just a ghastly, liquid-white and shimmering figure. It was, without question...a Ghost.

All three boys were frozen in their tracks. Trevor pissed his trousers, while Thomas soiled his.

Finally, Winston spoke. "God Almighty, have mercy on us."

The three were no longer drunk; they had been thoroughly and completely terrorized sober.

In retrospect, to break the barrier, ignoring an unambiguous administrative directive, was a rather foolish choice on their part. Yet, here they were.

The Ghost moved toward them. The light of the moon passed through a large, double-hung window, and its beams continued right through the apparition. Still, the boys did not budge.

The Ghost enveloped them. An arctic chill ran through every muscle and fiber of their beings, causing all three to tremble beyond belief.

The three would never be able to forget that humbling sensation. They would all forever recall the sense of dread, sorrow and soullessness filling their bodies.

The Ghost withdrew and raised its arm with clear contempt, directing them to leave, which they did, nearly wedging themselves in the doorway as they scrambled to escape. The Ghost pulled the door shut, locking itself against further entry.

The boys were then confronted by the night watchman who had been summoned by one of the third-floor occupants who had been awakened by the disturbance. Since the watchman had Trevor in an arm lock, the other two chose not to run.

Outside the building, the boys found their tongues and quickly recounted what had occurred.

Apparently, the watchman did not dispute their extraordinary tale. Rather, he calmly and forcefully said, "Come with me, lads. You need a warm fire, clean clothes and a spec of brandy. You'll sleep in my quarters tonight. Nothing to worry about. You'll be quite safe."

Sleep, they did not, but the next day, the three, along with the night watchman, appeared at 9:00 AM in the President's office in Mass Hall. President McKeen was waiting there, along with his new Dean of the College.

They listened intently to a full accounting, and then they asked the three to withdraw to the waiting room. There, the boys sat for something over an hour while deliberations took place in the President's office.

When they were asked to return, they entered with great fear – first from what they had experienced, and second, from thinking they would be permanently expelled for their stupid deeds.

President McKeen spoke clearly and slowly. "Gentlemen, last night you acted foolishly. Your conduct was unbecoming for Bowdoin men. You were drunk, in violation of our rules and the common law; you disobeyed a clear directive with respect to Winthrop Hall and deliberately violated the sanctity of a death site. Moreover, you destroyed property. For all this, the consequences would be to expel you from the College. Your parents would be notified and billed for all the damages. Disgrace would follow. No other respectable college or university would admit you after this, and your three years here would be for naught."

The President took in a deep breath and lowered his voice. "However, we are not going to do any of those things. We believe there are extenuating circumstances."

Trevor spoke up, "Sir, may I say something?"

"Hold your tongue, Mr. Trevor Wainwright. I am not finished, and you would be well-advised to stay silent until I conclude."

His icy glare sent shivers down the three young spines.

"We would certainly be justified in leveling these punishments, but, in fact, we will NOT."

These words were spoken with great emotion, and the boys definitely didn't miss the President's extra emphasis on the word "NOT".

President McKeen continued, "It is our belief that your delayed grief over the unfortunate Jonathan Edwards situation from last year caused you to drink in excess and then caused you to pay your respects to the dead lad's memory by gathering in his old room."

The President paused again, before continuing, "Now, Gentlemen, do I have that correct?"

Dumbfounded they were, but they all managed to get a "yes sir" out of their wide-open mouths.

President McKeen paused and then became somewhat harsh, "Now…as to what you think you saw or experienced, let me be unequivocally clear: it was and is a figment of the brew and your stupor. Your emotions over a tragic death and a full moon last night caused you to think you saw a ghost. But, lads, there are no such things as ghosts, now are there?"

Trevor started to disagree, then thought better of it and nodded his approval. The others followed suit.

"Now here's the deal, boys…first, this entire incident must never, and I repeat, NEVER, be repeated, discussed or shared with anyone – not your parents, your future wives or anyone else. Are we clear?"

"Yes," they all three quietly agreed.

"Secondly, you will never again enter Winthrop Hall for any reason at any time. And Never means NEVER! Thirdly, there is to be no diary, record or other writing about this incident. Agreed?"

Again, there followed a unified, affirmative response.

"Now here are the covenants, boys. We have prepared an agreement for you to sign. It recounts your behavior and your solemn agreement as I've outlined it. Should at any time, any one of you violate the covenant, the suspension will be put in place for all, your confessions will be published, and your degrees will be rescinded, resulting in disgrace and possible prosecution."

"May we discuss this, Sir?" Whispered Winston.

"No, you may not, Winston. You either sign your confession and covenant this instant, or we will proceed with your expulsion. And by the way, no one…and I mean no one…will ever believe your ridiculous ghost tale."

"Yes, sir. I'm ready to sign, Sir," Winston replied. The others did likewise.

Chapter 3

Over the years to come, all three kept their word. Trevor went to Harvard Law School and became a prosperous and highly-respected attorney and selectman. Thomas, the dullest of the three, pursued divinity graduate school and was ordained a Methodist minister. He was elevated to Bishop of the Boston Conference and enjoyed a most successful career along with a happy marriage to a beautiful, wealthy lass who bore him seven healthy, intelligent children.

Winston, unfortunately, upon graduation from Bowdoin, descended with unusual rapidity into a drunken, sinful life. He was well-known among the wharf rats of Portland Maine Harbor and could be seen around town scrounging for coins for a dime beer. Often, his ranting and ramblings recanted ghosts, but never the tale of The Ghost.

He was always cold and would have frozen to death one night at the old Port in Portland when he slipped, lost his footing, struck his head and disappeared from sight. Just before he descended into unconsciousness, Winston believed he saw The Ghost.

"You," he wailed. "You…it was true, not a figment." Then he passed out.

It would have been a tragic and premature death, but two sailors, hearing his cry, turned and were drawn to a lantern on the dock, a lantern that, mysteriously, was not on the dock previously. They discovered Winston's slumped body and took him to the hospital where he recovered...in spirit as well as body.

Believing The Ghost had saved his life for a purpose, Winston threw away his liquor bottles, his wanton ways and was born anew. For the next fifty-four years, he never touched a drop of alcohol and actually completed an illustrious teaching career, at none other than Bowdoin College.

More significantly, he worked tirelessly with alcoholic boys and young men, saving many a life by his actions.

Like his other cohorts from that fateful night, Winston never did breach his covenant of silence.

But as your narrator, I digress...

Chapter 4

1806
Returning to the office of Bowdoin's President...

At the conclusion of the signing of the covenant and the departure of the three students, President McKeen, Dean Smith and the night watchman all huddled around the President's great oak desk.

President McKeen thanked the watchman for his extraordinary diligence and continued discretion. He advised him that a substantial annual bonus would be forthcoming as well as a promotion, provided he kept the existence of this incident to himself.

The man thanked McKeen profusely and let himself out of his office.

"We'll never be able to suppress their story," lamented Dean Smith. "Those boys will never live up to the bargain. It will be all over the country. No one will come to a 'ghost college'. Bowdoin will lose its charter. We will be dismissed and disgraced. Ruin will follow us."

President McKeen shook his head. "You are quite wrong, Dean. Nothing of that sort is going to happen. Those boys will never utter a thing about this, mark my words. And as for our night watchman, he will never say anything about this either, and I'll tell you why...he will have a job here for the rest of his life and not as Night Watchman, but as Aide to the President, with a healthy raise in compensation."

This caused the Dean to feel slightly better, although he still doubted the silence of the three young men.

President McKeen continued, "We will not lock Room 208 anymore, but rather, we will seal it shut, completely eliminating any entrance for the remainder of this year. Over the summer, we will retool the second floor so that Room 208 will simply cease to exist, thusly eliminating it as a place of residence for our supposed apparition, which, of course, I do not believe exists. In any event, what does not exist cannot inhabit Room 208, for the room itself will not exist. Hopefully, this thing...ghost...whatever it is...will choose some other place to reside, far from our campus, I pray...Colby College perhaps."

Dean Smith was wide-eyed. "Do you honestly believe any of what you are saying, Sir? I can hardly believe my own ears."

McKeen glared at his Dean. "I believe every word I've said to you. The only thing I do not believe is that the damn thing was a ghost!"

Dean Smith winced. "Nevertheless, you will have to confide in our Board of Overseers, won't you? They must know the truth."

"And what is the truth?" President McKeen bellowed. "They will not be told about this by me...and certainly not by you. No one will be told!"

However, he thought to himself, I will record all of this in a diary, and it will be passed onto my successor, the next President of Bowdoin College. And I will very carefully secure such diary here at the College.

He paused in his thoughts, looked at Dean Smith's horrified face, but without saying more, continued reasoning out his actions in his own mind…

Yes, there is, in fact, a spirit at work here, and despite my prayer for its departure from Bowdoin, I fear this incident is only the beginning. Perhaps, though, this spirit may be a benevolent one; after all, the thing did not harm those three boys. Indeed, it may have scared them straight. But, I sense this is not an evil spirit. There is more to all of this than first appears.

And with that, McKeen dismissed his Dean and began recording his careful account of The Ghost of Bowdoin College in a black leather book with a brass lock on the front. Writing steadily for two solid hours, he finished the entire accounting. Then, he pondered as to the safest place to conceal this log.

Finally, he settled on an old white window bench in his office. For now, though, he would keep the diary with him at all times.

Given that he was a rather skilled carpenter in addition to a college president, over the next several weeks, after everyone had departed Mass Hall each evening, he personally crafted a secret compartment within the bench. It had a clever method of accessing such compartment, invisible to the uninformed. In the event of his sudden or unexpected death, only his wife would learn of the compartment and diary. She would be instructed to personally deliver a sealed letter to the next elected Bowdoin President.

The three students never broke the covenant, nor did Dean Smith ever mention the event to anyone in his lifetime. And the night watchman wasn't an issue either. Unfortunately, though, the latter never did get to see his promotion, for he used the first installment of his bonus money to purchase a case of the finest brandy and single malt scotch, which resulted in alcohol poisoning one night just three weeks after the incident.

Over the years, many more ghostly incidents would be recorded, but most of these occurred far from the Brunswick campus. The original diary was joined by others.

There were whispers, however, among the students and faculty about a ghost. But, in fact, nothing bad happened on the campus or anywhere else, so, in time, the whispers faded away...

Chapter 5

Franklin Pierce
1853
Andover, Massachusetts

The morning was especially cold. The kind of cold that cuts through your very soul. It was January 1853, so the weather was to be expected, yet, somehow, this was a different chill. It seemed to carry a message that danger was about. It was a day when you didn't really want to go outside. No...the message was more than that. It was warning you that you shouldn't go outside.

Franklin Pierce was not a superstitious man, so when he paused in his parlor room looking out the window, he ignored his instincts – namely that neither he nor his family should leave their warm abode.

His wife Jane Appleton Pierce and his sole surviving son Benjamin were both still asleep.

How much has happened in his life, he thought.

Jane was the daughter of Jesse Appleton, the second President of Bowdoin College, where he, Franklin, had graduated with the class of 1824. Such a period of great years at Bowdoin. Nathaniel Hawthorne and Henry

Wadsworth Longfellow in the class of 1825. And his now rival, John P. Hale, class of 1827.

Pierce had entered college when he was just fifteen years. Pretty young. He loved the place, but was somewhat a slow starter, finding himself, after two years, ranked at the very bottom of his class. But after that, he focused intensely on his studies. And his efforts paid off, as he graduated fifth in his very smart and distinguished class. Quite an accomplishment. Yet, this was nothing compared to the ensuing years.

He was elected to the New Hampshire State House, married Jane Appleton, had a successful law practice, was elected to the United States Senate and received a Presidential offer to become Attorney General of the United States, which he declined.

Then, the unthinkable happened at the wild Democratic National Convention of June 1852, when he emerged from nowhere to become the party's progressive nominee on the forty-ninth ballot. Despite his wife's grave misgivings about campaigns, Washington, D.C. and the "political life", Pierce soundly defeated his rival, General Winfield Scott and fellow alumnus John Hale.

All this went through the young President-elect's mind as he gazed out the window.

To be sure, there had been tragedy in his life. Two sons had both died early deaths, and only eleven-year-old Benjamin survived to carry on the Pierce legacy.

Benjamin was Franklin's pride and joy. He was a handsome young man and quite charming. He was as comfortable with adults as he was with children of his own age. You liked to be around him. All of which he had inherited from his famous father. Yet Benjamin was not affected. He didn't act like a privileged aristocrat, and he smiled and laughed often, frequently at himself.

Pierce was very proud of his son and happy that his wife had finally moved beyond the early deaths of their first two children.

But now, Franklin Pierce felt a bone-deep shiver rip through his body. Slowly, he turned from the window. There, in the parlor room, approximately ten feet from him was a gray apparition. Pierce blinked twice and attempted to refocus his vision. The apparition had completely formed. It became a young man, but without color or distinct outline.

It seemed to almost glide as it moved from the center of the room to a side table where the train tickets for today's journey to Concord, New Hampshire were lying on the table. The apparition, dare it be called a ghost, placed its hand on the three tickets and swept them from the table. The ghost seemed to be shaking its ungodly head, increasingly so until Pierce realized that the thing was warning him not to use the tickets.

The President-elect was frozen in his tracks. Time seemed to stand still.

Slowly, the ghost dissolved, and Pierce was left completely shaken. He instantly thought of the old rumors about The Ghost of Bowdoin College. Like the other students, he had heard the stories and joined the laughter, joking about the mythical ghost.

But what just happened here, he wondered. *What was this? Why are my train tickets on the floor?*

At that very moment, Jane called out to him, and Pierce answered her. Bending to pick up the tickets, he placed them inside his suit pocket and climbed upstairs to the bedroom.

Franklin Pierce chose to put this experience out of his mind. It's the stress and pressure of all that's been happening, he thought. I haven't had breakfast and ate too little at dinner last night. Perhaps I am experiencing an eating disorder causing me to imagine things. He convinced himself it wasn't real.

At approximately 11 AM, Franklin Pierce, his wife Jane and son Benjamin all headed to the Boston & Maine Train. They were exactly on schedule as was the train.

The family accepted the congratulations and good wishes of the fellow passengers and train conductors which were bound to be bestowed upon the President-elect of the United States of America.

After settling into their private compartment, Benjamin began recounting his prior day's adventure in Boston. He was excited, happy, full of boyish enthusiasm and had his parents laughing with him as he described the trip he'd been on with his friend Michael and tutor Thomas Graughcly to the home of Paul Revere, in Boston's north end.

About twenty minutes into the journey, the entire train screeched and shook violently. An enormous branch of a towering oak tree had fallen across the train tracks, and the engineer had not been able to stop the locomotive in time to avoid crashing head first into the obstruction. The train buckled, causing the fourth passenger car to disengage from its connection and topple over an embankment, sliding some twenty-five feet down the slope.

It all happened so quickly, no one, including The Pierces, had time to do anything except grab onto the nearest thing within reach.

Young Benjamin lunged toward the compartment door, when the unspeakable happened. The car toppled onto its side, throwing him out the window with the car crushing him.

Before his very eyes, Franklin Pierce, the soon to be Fourteenth President of the United States, watched his son's decapitation. His wife mercifully had been knocked unconscious, but Pierce was fully-awake and horrified.

All he could think of at that moment was the morning incident. *It was warning me. It was telling me not to go on this train. But, I didn't heed the warning.* This is my fault, he cried to himself.

Of course, this terrible accident was not the fault of Franklin Pierce, but he would never be the same. He was forever changed and in ways we cannot imagine or describe. He, indeed, became President, and his four years' time in the Presidency was marked with many unfortunate calamities and poor decisions, ultimately setting the stage for the War Between the States, the ultimate disaster.

Pierce's old friend Nathaniel Hawthorne mourned for him, but there was nothing he could do. The path had been set.

We can only speculate what might have been had Franklin Pierce heeded the apparent warning he had been given by an apparent "ghost."

Chapter 6

Joshua Chamberlain
July 2, 1863
Gettysburg Little Round Top

Col. Joshua Lawrence Chamberlain, 34 years, recent Professor of Rhetoric at Bowdoin College, now on leave, the newly-appointed leader of the 20th Maine Regiment, found himself alone and at wits end in his tent at Little Round Top, Gettysburg, Pennsylvania. His brother Tom entered with sweat streaming down his face.

"Joshua, we must pull back," Tom said. "I've checked twice. Our ammunition is depleted, depleted I tell you. We are sitting ducks for Lee's men. They are going to storm up the Hill any minute. We'll be slaughtered. Give the order, Brother, give the order now!"

Chamberlain heard him. But, General Meade specifically told him to hold his position at all costs. He wondered, for a moment, how his brother and he had come to this point in their lives. They were a very long way from the familiar grounds of their Maine homeland.

It's true, he thought, we have no more ammunition. The regiment can't possibly hold this hill. And when we are overrun, the Confederates will outflank General Meade; we will lose this battle and maybe the entire campaign. I can't believe it is to be my fate – my failure – that will cause our Northern armies to be defeated.

"Tom, I hear you. Go outside...please. I need a moment to think."

Tom Chamberlain looked hard at his brother. He loved Joshua very much, but right now, he thought his brother was absolutely crazy, and God forbid, frozen with fear. It had to be one or the other.

No bullets. They had no bullets. They had no conceivable way to stop the deadly assault just minutes away. They had to pull out, or they would all be killed. Didn't Joshua know this better than anyone?

"Joshua," Tom pleaded.

"Please, Tom. I ask you...give me a moment."

Tom Chamberlain turned his back on his brother, but he would only do so for the single minute Joshua asked of him and then he would pull him, forcibly if necessary, out of that tent and away from the coming hellfire.

Joshua stared into the flame in front of him then felt a presence from behind. Slowly, with a sense of dread, he turned.

He was staring at a gray mass, and it was taking the distinct shape of a young man right before his eyes. The mass pointed at Chamberlain's rifle and the bayonet fixed along to it then wrapped what appeared to be his hand around the bayonet.

In that instant, Joshua knew what he had to do, and the second he knew, the mass was gone.

Joshua arose with steely determination and exited his tent. As he began to step through the opening, the Confederates began their assault up the slope, firing at will. In a split second, a bullet pierced his coat. Two more inches

~ 26 ~

to the left, and he would have been dead. But he wasn't. He was alive. Very alive. And transfixed.

His brother was excited to see him but was also frightened by the look in his eyes.

"Fix bayonets," Joshua Chamberlain shouted.

Tom ran to him. "What are you doing, Joshua?! We must retreat!"

Joshua slowly turned toward his brother, and in a voice that sounded not his own, boomed over Tom. "Soldiers of the Northern Army of the Potomac, loyal men of the 20th Maine Regiment, hear me and act accordingly. Fix Bayonets! We are attacking these rebels and will drive them deep into God's own earth. Fix Bayonets! Now!"

With that, and somehow infused with a rush of new adrenalin, the soldiers of the North whipped into action with an indescribable fury, attaching their 8-inch long, steel knives to their bullet-less rifles, willing themselves forward, screaming at the top of their lungs.

The sight of all these wild men hurling themselves down the precipice of Little Round Top, the spectacle of their weapons of death and their bloodcurdling Yankee chorus froze every Confederate in his tracks.

The rebel soldiers either dropped their weapons in supplicate surrender or turned tail and ran as fast as they could back down the slopes.

On July 2nd of 1863, Joshua Chamberlain won the battle at Little Round Top. Many historians believe that this was the turning point of the Battle of Gettysburg and, in fact, the entire Civil War. Had Little Round Top fallen, Lee could undoubtedly have won Gettysburg decisively and threatened the very existence of Washington D.C. which

Lincoln may have avoided only by negotiating a truce –
resulting in two Americas.

But…that is not what happened…

Chapter 7

Robert Peary
1877
Bowdoin College

Robert E. Peary was one of Bowdoin College's most tenacious seniors. He was bright, hard-working and zealous in achieving his objectives. His grades reflected this, and his professors predicted he would accomplish great things in the years to come.

This particular evening, however, Peary was sitting in a corner of the living room of Delta Kappa Epsilon listening intently to his fellow Deke fraternity brothers. They were a fun-loving group of extremely athletic young men, and for the most part, the Dekes liked Peary, especially his intense ability to focus. Occasionally, though, they also found him to be a somewhat boastful pain in the ass. Tonight was turning out to be a time reflecting all of these qualities.

During Friday night's typical revelry, the talk had turned to the numerous unsuccessful attempts which had been made to scale the Bowdoin Chapel spire. A few had attempted this most dangerous feat, but no one had ever come close to reaching the pinnacle. Not the crazy Chi Psi nor the macho Sigma Nus nor even the zany Zetas.

Now, as the beer in the half keg fell precipitously near the "empty" mark, Peary spoke out in that clear commanding voice of his, "Gents, if scaling were truly worth the effort, it not only could be done, but I, myself, could do it this very night. You see, it's a combination of applied physics and physical strength."

Without hesitating, he went on, "I not only possess the knowledge of how to do it, but clearly have the physical means to carry it off. But be clear on this...I've not about the larks, no matter how much ale is involved."

A stunned group of twenty or so boisterous Dekes were brought to complete and utter silence. It was as if time had suspended itself while these young men processed Peary's incredible statement. He was claiming he could scale the spire, and that he could do it this very evening.

"Impossible," several shouted, breaking the silence.

"I tell you it can be done, and I can do it, but I will not do so just to satisfy your immature and undeveloped minds. There must be a suitable prize and, of course, the fame that goes with accomplishing a seemingly un-accomplishable task."

A flood of catcalls and hissing were unleashed. Peary, however, stood his ground.

"I will do this," he bellowed, "but must receive $500 for the lessons you'll be taught – not a penny less."

The gauntlet having been thrown in the faces of these macho fraternity men, complete bedlam broke out. Notwithstanding that, in 1877, $500 was a virtual fortune, the "word" went out throughout the fraternity house, and all thirty-seven brothers pooled their financial resources as well as authorized a "loan" of $250 from the Deke Treasury Reserve Fund.

Peary, satisfied that, indeed, the prize money had been assembled, said, "It is now five minutes to eight o'clock. At precisely 11 PM, you are to assemble at the Chapel to witness a Bowdoin milestone. And don't forget the money!"

Peary then retired to his room where he had already assembled the necessary gear. He had thought about the spire for some time. In fact, he was sure he had calculated the exact way to scale the tower and reach the needlepoint tip. He also desperately needed the money.

Quickly, but without rushing so fast that he might forget something, he assembled his tools and changed into the clothes he had ascertained would be suitable for such a dangerous feat. The most important of these were the unusual shoes which he had crafted in Boston and shipped to himself several weeks ago.

Everything was in complete readiness as he went over the details in his mind. For weeks, he had silently and precisely made his visits to the chapel and meticulously performed his calculations. After all, his engineering prowess was almost as legendary on campus as his bull-headed determination.

But like so many things in our lives, Peary wasn't undertaking this dangerous dare for ego alone. No, it was much more practical.

He needed the money, which was a small fortune, in order to quiet an increasingly annoying young lass with whom he had engaged in numerous, secret dalliances from the town of Brunswick…all unknown to his fraternity brothers and the Bowdoin College Administration, with the exception of his faithful roommate Richard Charles Stedman.

Stedman was watching over him as he made his preparations. "Peary, why are you risking your life for this?

Why, why Peary? You have so much going for you. This dare means nothing. Don't do it man! For the love of God, don't do it!"

Peary replied, "Richard, you are a dear friend, one of the truest, but you just don't understand me."

"Rubbish, Peary! I understand you all too well. It's about the girl...the Townie, isn't it? You've figured out a way to get her a lot of money...$500...that's what it will take to shut her up, isn't it? Admit it."

"I admit no such thing," Peary intoned, "and as far as the girl is concerned, she is a figment of your overactive imagination."

Stedman sadly shook his head. Peary was his hero, a granite rock of grit, smarts and steady resolve, but he certainly had his Achilles' heel and that was Woman!

At the stroke of 11 PM, Peary, with faithful Stedman at his side, confidently strode into the foreground of the venerable chapel. Some two hundred Bowdoin men were silently assembled in the increasingly foggy night, including every brother of Deke fraternity.

William Chastington, Deke President, stepped forward with the envelope of bills. "Peary, as promised, here is the prize, if you can safely achieve the pinnacle and claim the wager. Of course, there's still time for you to come to your senses, confess you've had too much to drink, and we'll all return to our rooms.

"The devil you will," Peary barked. "Now stand clear."

Peary moved with the swiftness of a cat and the eye of a tiger. He entered the chapel through the unlocked door. Then he moved to the southwest corner where stairs led up to a small window with access to the spire.

Next, he slid part-way through the window to get a foot on the ledge beneath the pinnacle. From his rump sack, he pulled out a small crossbow with a grappling hook at the tip of a sturdy steel arrow. He took aim and released the missile, which carried straight and true to the base of the pinnacle and secured itself.

During this time, the fog thickened, rapidly reducing any real visibility. Peary pulled himself fully out the window and leaned against the granite wall. He carefully tested the grappling line and then felt for a handhold in the uneven stones.

He tentatively tested his special shoes and found them gripping solidly. He extended his arm and felt for another handhold. Satisfied, he used his incredible strength to begin pulling himself up.

Below, the crowd sighted him and gave a collective gasp as they witnessed him begin his ascent.

Once he was about thirty-five feet high, he was increasingly less visible to the crowd below, who were straining their eyes to follow his progress. With each additional foot of climb, he became even harder to see.

As he reached about sixty feet, he suddenly felt an icy chill. Instantly, he sensed a presence. He had, of course, heard all the stories of a Bowdoin ghost, but he was too much of an engineer and scientist to put any stock in such tall tales. He thought they were the figments of silly men who consumed too much beer.

Yet, here he was, some sixty feet in the air, and a damn ghost chose this moment to appear to him. He was staring right at the thing. He knew that his senses were not deceiving him. He clearly saw an apparition. This was something extraordinary. And if he wasn't hanging sixty feet above a very hard surface, he might have enjoyed the experience.

In the distance, he could hear cheering from his Bowdoin brothers below, urging him on. Yet, the apparition motioned for him to go back.

For the very first time in his young life, Robert E. Peary felt fear. Funny thing about fear, though, is it does crazy things to the human body and mind.

Sensing his impenetrable, steely nerves coming apart, Peary broke out in a cold sweat. He took a deep breath, shook his fist at the apparition and hissed, "I don't believe in ghosts. You are just the fog."

At that point, he wasn't very far from the top of the spire, but he felt his grappling hook move. This was a big problem. If he exerted more upward pressure on the line, he would very likely fall to his death.

He quickly looked down, noticing that the fog obscured the view from below. He had now reached one of those pesky, ethical crossroads in life: either he could admit he came close, but failed to reach the summit, or he could claim victory, win the desperately needed money and go on.

In that brief moment, Peary chose his path. He took off his cap, aimed and flung it high. As if guided by an unforeseen force, the cap caught on the top of the needlepoint spire.

Peary yelled to the men below, "I've done it! I've reached the top, and to prove it, I've placed my cap atop the Bowdoin Chapel spire."

Quickly, he descended, without his anchor hook moving further. Again, as if there were divine intervention, the fog lifted enough so that the crowd below could plainly see his cap atop the spire. They cheered madly. When he exited from the ground level door, there were thunderous hurrays and much backslapping all-around.

Even the night watchman who had joined the crowd congratulated him, "Mr. Peary, I don't know how you did it, but that's your cap up there, and I didn't see a thing."

Peary was awarded the prize money. For those few doubting Thomases, the next morning, they reassembled in front of the chapel, and sure enough, there hung Peary's cap atop the highest point of the spire for all the world to witness. There was no doubt now. Peary had done it.

Not the danger, the apparent impossibility, nor even a ghost could stop this man. Surely, this was someone who would make his mark in the world in the years to come.

April 6, 1909
Approximately 5 miles from the North Pole

Admiral Robert E. Peary knew this was his final expedition. For almost a quarter century, he had been obsessed with reaching the North Pole. All the years of preparation, the expeditions, the planning and the controversies had brought him to this moment. He was finally within reach.

His party had left New York City's harbor on the SS Roosevelt. They'd overcome many challenges to reach this point. However, Peary had only a few men remaining, and they were all exhausted.

His Bowdoin education prepared him well for the Artic tribulations. At that moment, however, he was thinking back to the night he scaled the Bowdoin Chapel spire. That feat, such as it was, not only sealed his campus reputation, but gave him the means to make a pushy, bothersome townie girl, with whom he'd had a fling, go away. If only the situation with the Inuits were as simple.

Unfortunately, Peary's detractors and rivals were claiming that both he and his erstwhile loyal companion Matthew Henson, had what can be described as "intimate relations" with native Inuit tribal women and, further, that Peary's mistress had become pregnant. So far, Peary had managed to stave them off, but for how much longer, no one knew for sure.

Certainly, it would be extraordinarily difficult to raise the financial support for another expedition if this one failed. Either he reached 90 degrees N now, or it was utter failure.

Fatigue was building within this lion of a man; the weather was worsening and not even the dogs could go. For the moment, he was alone in his tent, while the other men were around the fire. It seemed unerringly quiet.

Thinking back to the moment he scaled the Bowdoin Chapel spire, a familiar chill came over him. He looked up and saw The Ghost in front of him once more, pointing to his map. Slowly, but distinctly, the spirit traced the return route to Peary's ship. In effect, the ghost was telling him to turn back, just like it had advised him to do at Bowdoin.

The apparition then moved its finger ahead to the map marker for the pole and, dramatically, the paper burned a circular hole right at 90 degrees. The spirit was telling Peary that if he forged on, he would perish.

And then it was gone, as if it had never been there, at all. Was Peary imagining things, caused by exhaustion, the blistering cold and hunger? He walked outside and looked at his companions. *Should I risk their lives?*

"It's insane to think I actually experienced a ghost now any more than the time at Bowdoin College," he muttered under his breath. "But then again, what really happened at Bowdoin?"

While his fellow hearty souls all peered at him, their leader, trying to decide what was going thru his mind, Peary made his decision…

History would credit him for achieving great things, but to this day, there is intense debate as to whether he actually reached the North Pole. The question is whether he did, indeed, heed the spirit's warning and turn back while at the same time claiming victory, or did he forge ahead for the remaining few miles to achieve True North.

Perhaps only The Ghost knows for certain...

Chapter 8

Vincent Mark
2009
The New York Stock Exchange, New York City

The morning was crisp, the air breathable. At 8:30 AM, the New York Stock Exchange was alive with financial people, brokers, traders, runners and more streaming in from the great island of Manhattan, the lessor boroughs as well as the burbs around Manhattan, all scurrying to the highest floors.

Their routines were remarkably similar: all of them, men and women alike, downed steaming-hot, black coffee with hard-buttered rolls, most from the Puerto Rican girl in the mobile coffee cart on the ground level. The "suits" had already powered up their computers, scrolled through a hundred emails or so and were pumping themselves up for big action.

One could feel the energy surging through the entire area. It was exciting! Stimulating. Almost sexual. For many of the guys and gals, it was better than sex, or at least the sex they were having. Here, they were alive and, with every passing minute, their entire being was acutely aware that there was a lot of money to be made. Lots and lots of money.

Of course, you could lose just as much money, but hey, this was Wall Street. These were smart, aggressive people, with street savvy and major guts – all looking for an edge and grabbing it whenever they could. Often, though, the edge was a foolish place to be. And they knew that, too.

At exactly thirteen minutes past noon on this day, Vincent Mark, a Bowdoin College graduate, lawyer and recently admitted member of the New York State Bar Association, turned right off Wall Street onto Broad Street to enter the New York Stock Exchange. He was perilously close to being late for an important meeting with senior people from The Exchange about a "dream" job.

But just as he passed through the revolving doors, something drew his attention to the outside southern wall. It appeared to be a jet-black bird with piercing eyes.

Vincent stopped. He couldn't explain it, but he was irresistibly drawn to the bird. He quickly retraced his steps back through the lobby and out the revolving door, never taking his eyes off the creature.

As he exited the building and headed toward the bird, it lifted slowly into the air and flew toward the southwest corner of the structure. At precisely that moment, Vincent Mark lowered his eyes from the bird to a metamorphic image shimmering below it. The image held out one of its arms, clearly motioning Vincent away from the building.

In this metropolis of millions, in the shadow of one of the busiest venues in the city of New York, he could not believe that no one, save himself, was witnessing this incredible vision.

The next second, Vincent found his feet moving almost of their own volition, and he was running in the direction of the ghostly image which was rapidly melting away.

It was now 12:17 PM, and because of Vincent's hurried entrance and sudden, rather bizarre exit, New York City police and security personnel were immediately focused on the front entrance and drawn to the spot where a man was pulling an automatic weapon from under his coat.

Fortunately, they acted with incredible speed and apprehended the gunman without shots being fired. Very fortunate for Vincent, too, who otherwise would have been directly in the kill zone.

While Vincent did not get the job that day, he never would have seen a paycheck had he not been led away from the lobby.

Chapter 9

Frank Dubois
April 23, 2012
New Rochelle, New York

Frank Dubois was an excellent Chief Financial Officer. His credentials included a Columbia undergraduate degree, an MBA from Harvard Business School and the fact that he had passed his CPA Exam, all parts, on the first attempt. This was no mean feat, in and of itself, but more significantly, he scored the highest grade ever achieved on the examination in over sixty years.

While toiling diligently at Arthur Andersen for some seven years, Frank rose thru the ranks from Senior to Manager to Partner. He would have had quite a career at Andersen, but his work ethic didn't match his intellect. Instead of sixteen-hour work days, Frank, with a wife and three kids, opted for a position with one of his firm's clients, The Sterling Works, an old, but rather sleepy company headquartered in the Manhattan borough of New York City. He was their CFO. The pay was very good, the hours were reasonable, and life was quite manageable.

Today, however, the members of the Finance Department had been pulling together the numbers for the so-called 3rd Run for the quarter ending March 31. It took three separate computer inputs and complete computations to produce accurate financials for the period, with checking, rechecking and review. The results had been acceptable, if not good. Nothing flashy, just like the company. The Sterling Works would meet, not exceed, Wall Street's expectations for the first quarter, and there would be no change to the full-year estimate. It was sort of like kissing your sister.

At 9:38 PM, Frank was on his way to his home in New Rochelle, southern Westchester County. He decided on the spur of the moment to stop off at the Purple Tavern on Division Street. It was a regular haunt of his.

The bartender instantly recognized him as he passed through the door. By the time he reached the bar, his Glenlivet neat was poured and waiting for him. Single malt scotch, Frank thought, was Scotland's great gift to the civilized world.

Although a pretty, flirtatious young blond, with a short skirt and great legs, tried to engage him in conversation, he begged off and downed his drink. Just one, he thought, that's all I want or need. He left a twenty-dollar bill on the bar and headed out to his S-8 Audi in the side parking lot.

As he fumbled with his keys, Frank didn't see the tall man with a full-length leather trench coat silently slide up to him.

"Give me your wallet and your watch," the man hissed. "Now."

Frank whirled around, dropping his keys in the process.

"What?" He stammered.

"You heard me…your wallet and your watch," the man repeated.

The thief was well-over six-feet-tall with an athletic build, dark glasses and a plain baseball cap pulled down low. The gun in his right hand was sixteen inches from Frank's stomach and looked very real.

He sure didn't look like a street mugger, Frank thought, but, if not a practical fellow, he was a very savvy New Yorker. His Baume & Mercier watch was insured, and there was about $500 cash in his wallet – a cheap price to avoid a bullet, and, the credit cards, of course, could be replaced.

Quickly, he complied, handing over both items to the scary-looking stranger, while silently cursing himself for indulging in the pitstop for the scotch.

"I should have driven straight home to Martha," he muttered.

Of course, many a man has uttered those words after regretting an improvised night out.

Unfortunately, those were Frank's last words ever…

In one, swift motion of his arm, the trench coat man raised his gun and fired a single, .22-caliber bullet dead center into Frank's heart. In a mere ninety-three seconds from the time he exited the Purple Tavern, his life was over. Just like that.

The killer bent over and fired a second bullet into Frank's right arm. Never looking around to see if he'd been spotted, he walked away.

Two other men, strategically placed at corners of the parking lot, were carefully and professionally scanning the area for potential witnesses. There were none. They, too, melted into the night.

Frank Dubois, 44-years-old, a faithful husband and father of three, was to become another sidewalk statistic in New York's crime reports. He would be recorded as the victim of a random, meaningless mugging.

It was sad that Frank was buried, with a grieving wife and children, tearful friends and distraught colleagues, never knowing it made no difference that he stopped off for a drink that night.

His wallet and watch were later discarded into a commercial trash compactor, ultimately ending up in a waste disposal site in New Jersey.

The bitter reality was that Frank Dubois had been a marked man, and, like a lot of things in life, he never knew it.

Chapter 10

Maria and John Esposito
April 25, 2012
Staten Island, New York

Maria Delvecchio Esposito was a full-blooded Sicilian. Both her father and mother we born and raised in Siracusa, Sicily, located on the southeastern coast of that serpent island which is part of Italy.

Maria's parents were married at eighteen and immigrated to the United States when they were twenty. Her brother, Salvatore, was born shortly thereafter, and Maria followed two years later. She and her brother were both raised in strict Sicilian fashion. Maria went to mass every day. Her marinara sauce was to die for, and she could sing every Verdi opera the great man ever composed. Both Delvecchio children were extremely bright, and Maria graduated summa cum laude from Salve Regina University in Newport, Rhode Island.

While a freshman in college, she met John Esposito, who was then a senior at Brown University. They dated sporadically that year, but it wasn't until some years later, after John had graduated from Columbia Law and completed a successful tour at the Wall Street law firm Black & Lace, that they married.

John's roots traced from Reggio Calabria in the southern-most province of Italy. Maria's parents were thrilled with the union. Her brother, however, was less enthusiastic. He was extremely protective of his sister and had carefully and thoroughly checked out John's history – not so much his professional career as his sex life.

John was extremely good looking, charming and bright. He also possessed the infamous, Calabrian male sex gene which meant he was perpetually horny. This was either a blessing or a curse, depending on your viewpoint. Before marrying Maria, he had a notorious string of romances. Salvatore also learned that as a result of these many affairs, John may have impregnated a woman, which, in turn, was followed by a hasty and quiet abortion.

Salvatore had done everything in his power to dissuade his sister from marriage.

At 38 years, Maria Delvecchio was still drop dead gorgeous. When she entered a room, every man drooled over her voluptuous figure, while every woman hated her for her stunning beauty.

"Nothing good will come from this marriage, Maria, he will be unfaithful," screamed Salvatore, the evening before the ceremony. "This Calabrian is not to be trusted. He will bring you nothing but heartbreak and misery."

"You do not know Giovanni as I do, Salvatore. You are wrong about him," Maria said.

At the time of their nuptials, John Esposito was 41-years-old and had served as General Counsel for The Sterling Works for the past two-and-a-half years. Maria Esposito had just turned 38, but she was a virgin. Almost unheard of anywhere in the United States, these days, but quite true.

The couple had now been married less than eight months. The pent-up years of abstinence exploded on their wedding night, and after a short, but intense debate, Maria was intent on bringing a child into the world, even at her somewhat late age.

On a beautiful April day, in the late afternoon, she was standing in her massive, ultra-modern kitchen, bent over a large sauce pan, pouring olive oil and quietly humming from the Verdi opera "*La Forza del Destino*".

She did not hear the tall man dressed in black slide up behind her, although in that second, before his hands closed around her beautiful mouth, Maria's Sicilian senses alerted her to danger. Sadly, it was too late.

As her arms were pinned behind her back by two additional intruders, similarly clothed in black, she could not scream. While furiously struggling to escape her captors, her mind raced with a stream of thoughts. *Why didn't I hear anything? What do they want? Are they here to rob the house or rape me?*

Before she could organize her stream of consciousness any further, she was whirled around and then suddenly released. In the same instant, she saw a large .22-caliber pistol inches from her temple.

The gun fired, and her life ended. Just like that.

After her killers allowed her body to slump to the floor, a deep, red pool of blood immediately collected around her. The tall man then walked to the stove, shut off the flame and carefully emptied the contents of the pan into a large, black plastic bag. The incidentals on the counter were returned to their cabinets. The three men pulled out chairs, checked their watches and silently waited.

Approximately one hour later, John Esposito arrived home, unlocked the front door and with a smile on his face, strode confidently into his home. As he came face-to-face with the intruders and the same pistol, his smile turned to shock. The silenced gun fired and struck him to the left of his heart. A second, third and fourth bullet penetrated his entire front.

He was moved to the kitchen, his body arranged opposite Maria's, the men carefully arranging her so that the pistol was gripped in her hand, and she was slumped to the side.

The tall man placed a yellow rose over John's chest, which now leaked profusely. The yellow rose, a symbol of infidelity, would be clearly understood in the Italian community.

Chapter 11

Thursday, April 26, 2012
Westchester County, New York

At 9:18 Thursday morning, Vincent Mark was pushing 70 on the Hutchinson River Parkway in his 1978 MGB with the top down in late Spring's absolute splendor. His new Phantom radar detector warned him of any potential police speed traps and would block their signals, or at least that's what it advertised it could do.

As he sped his way to Boston to round with a few Bowdoin College buddies, Vincent wanted no problems. He had taken a couple of rare vacation days from his job at The Sterling Works as Associate General Counsel.

While NPR classical radio was on a commercial break, he checked the news on WINS. "You give us twenty minutes, and we'll give you the world".

What he heard almost caused him to veer off the highway.

The newscaster was detailing a tragic crash of a private airline at 8 AM that morning. All five souls, including two crew, were killed. The jet was carrying the Chairman, Chief Executive Officer & Chief Operating Officer of The

Sterling Works. There had not been a corporate air disaster this bad since Texasgulf Inc. in the 80's.

My God, Vincent thought, this was his company! These were people he had worked with every day for the last several years. Nausea overcame him. Then came guilt. He was scheduled to be on that flight!

He pulled off the highway as soon as he was able to safely. Hitting the speed dial for his office on his Samsung, his heart pounded. The call rang straight through to his assistant. She answered the phone crying.

"My God, Marsha, what happened?!"

"Vincent, it's awful," she managed to say between sobs. "We just got the news here via a special bulletin on all the TV stations. I can't believe it...Mr. Carradine, Mr. Winchester and Mr. Van Epps, all of them are dead, Vincent...dead. Why? How? I don't understand this. Nothing makes sense to me anymore. First, Mr. Dubois was mugged and murdered, then the whole Esposito situation and now this plane crash. I have chills. Vincent, I know that you were going to fly with them. If your plans hadn't changed, you would be dead right now."

Vincent Mark hadn't thought much about dying, as most of us don't either. In fact, dying is a thing we consciously avoid contemplating. That is, until we are dying...or are about to...or...when we have a near miss.

Vincent's mind traveled at warped speed. Dozens of thoughts flooded his head.

"Vincent, Vincent, are you there? Please answer me."

Vincent snapped back into reality, as cars whizzed by him, oblivious to his plight.

"Vincent, there's more," Marsha said. "Just as the bulletin on the plane crash hit the news, we were served with a Schedule 13D. Someone is launching a hostile takeover of our company."

"What?!" Vincent yelled. "Are you kidding me, Marsha? A takeover? Who? How?"

Marsha could barely get out the words, her crying approaching an uncontrollable stage. "Vincent, I don't know anything except that you need to get back here. Everyone is hysterical over the crash and this takeover on top of it. Please, please hurry!"

Vincent pushed his vintage MGB as fast as he dared. He didn't care about getting a speeding ticket; he simply couldn't afford the time it would take to generate it. By the time he reached 34th and Park, Sterling Works' headquarters, his head was about to explode.

He couldn't begin to process the tragic events of the past twenty-four hours. How, why and what were all questions churning through his brain. He pulled into the parking garage on 34th and catapulted out of his convertible.

He flipped his keys to Juan, the attendant, who said, "Hey, Mr. Mark, I'm real sorry about that plane crash this morning, but do you believe the latest news? There was just another flash bulletin on WINS. It seems your Mr. Esposito was shot to death by his wife who then killed herself. Looks like she found out he was cheating on her. Man, you guys are having some really bad shit. You better be real careful, Mr. Mark. It's a good thing you aren't married. We don't want some broad putting a .22-caliber in you, no disrespect to the dead, mind you."

Vincent felt his blood pressure spike like a supercharged vette. He grabbed the railing in front of him before collapsing into Juan's plastic chair in front of the small garage office.

Vincent Mark was a young man in utter turmoil. His entire world had just crashed around him. Yet, he was too young to consider all this a random turn of the screw.

Vincent had always strived for control, for routine, or at least a semblance of order in his life, like all of us, really.

At this instant, nothing made sense to him. All these tragedies were happening at once, as if the Seven Seals of the Apocalypse were breaking at the same time.

He kept breathing deeply, just as his old soccer coach drilled into him whenever his nerves began to ignite during an intense game. He rose from the wobbly chair and thanked Juan profusely for his support. Then he headed for the elevator, stepping inside with a much firmer grip on his emotions, though his mind was still racing.

Mercifully, there was no one else inside, so he could continue breathing deep, using the calming technique he knew well, without embarrassment.

Just before the cab reached its destination, however, he sensed a presence, though no one was there with him.

Am I losing my mind?

In that nanosecond, he witnessed The Ghost and shivered. It was only for a few seconds, but he knew what he saw, and oddly, the bizarre event calmed him more.

The elevator came to a stop on the 24th floor – the main reception area for The Sterling Works, Vincent stepped out and started to head past the receptionist to his office when a young lady stepped abruptly in front of him.

"Mr. Mark? Mr. Vincent Mark?"

"Yes," he said as he stopped and focused on the young woman. She was attractive, very attractive in fact, with dark hair and dark eyes, and she was wearing an extremely flattering suit.

Amazing how in the midst of a mega crisis, the male sex gene kicks in. It seems that no matter what personal chaos a man is struggling with, the male animal never ignores the lure of the female. It rarely seems to work the other way though. Females somehow maintain self-control. Is the female gender more evolved? Could the male species be the lesser animal?

None of these philosophical questions were racing thru Vincent's head, mind you, not that he would admit anyway, but they remain for the rest of us to ponder, nonetheless.

"Yes, I'm Vincent Mark," he said, wanting to get to his office but also wanting to know what this beautiful woman wanted from him.

The woman held out her hand and said smoothly without any pretense, "My name is Angela Dominica. I'm with the New York State Attorney General's Office, and I'm an Assistant Attorney General."

"I'm sorry, Ms. Domenic —"

"Miss Dominica," she quickly corrected.

The correction was not lost upon Vincent, in spite of his overtaxed brain.

"I'm sorry, Miss Dominica, but I am in the middle of a crisis here."

"Yes, Mr. Mark, I'm quite aware of your crisis, and that is why I'm here. My boss is Albert Travaine, the Attorney General of the State of New York. He was a long-time friend of your COO, Mr. Van Epps. Attorney General Travaine sent me here to express his deep regrets and most sincere sympathy, as well as to offer any, and all, assistance our office can extend to The Sterling Works and its employees."

As Vincent walked with Ms. Dominica to his office, he was abruptly interrupted by Sterling Works' surefooted Office Manager, Katherine Dudley.

"Mr. Mark," she snapped, "I need to see you immediately, as in right now!"

Her tone could chill an ice cube and was delivered without her ever glancing at the attractive interloper accompanying Vincent. He was taken aback by Dudley's strident tone and rigid body language. Even by her everyday twisted nature, clearly, there was something very wrong.

He turned to Ms. Dominica and said, "I'm sorry, I appreciate the AG's condolences and kindness, and I'm sure his office can assist us in any number of ways. However, under the circumstances, I wonder if we could meet later. If it's not inappropriate, I'd be willing to buy you dinner."

Without hesitation, she replied, "Actually, that would work quite well…with the clear understanding that we split the cost of dinner. The Attorney General's Office has strict rules."

Vincent smiled and said, "Good. Shall we say 9 PM at Il Mulino?"

"Sounds perfect. I know the restaurant, of course, and will see you there." With that, she shook Vincent's hand, holding it just a second longer than necessary, before executing a flawless turn on her four-inch stilettos and gracefully exiting.

Vincent admired the beauty of it all.

"Mr. Mark." It was the indomitable Dudley again. "May we talk in your office?" She asked, all the while leading the way, pausing only briefly to open the door to his office before marching inside.

Vincent stepped forward into his small corporate domain and settled into his chair. He knew what was coming would not be a "talk" but rather a lecture.

Dudley immediately dove in, "Vice Chairman Shore has been calling constantly for you the past ninety-four minutes, and I don't think you should be wasting your time with some pretty young Assistant AG when death is all around us and our beloved company is under attack. This certainly is not the behavior I would expect —"

At that point, Vincent rose from his chair and cut her off mid- sentence. He'd had enough. His emotions were raw, and he just couldn't stomach a Dudley diatribe right now, no matter how right she might be.

"Ms. Dudley, why don't you get Mr. Shore on the telephone for me this very moment? Thank you so much."

Vincent turned toward the window, thereby signaling their "talk" was over. With that, Dudley pivoted on her right foot and stormed out the door, heading for her phone. Within seconds, she had Leonard Shore on the line.

"Vincent, thanks for getting back to me promptly," Shore began. "Things are really a mess. You obviously know about the plane crash." It was a statement, not a question.

"Yes, I do."

"But do you know about this business with Esposito?" This was a question, not a statement.

"Yes again, Leonard. I just learned about it, although I can't believe that John's wife would shoot him and then herself. My God, what is going on?! I don't understand any of this," Vincent said and stammered, searching for answers he didn't have.

"Neither do I, Vincent," Shore said. "Although, Maria was Sicilian, and there have always been rumors about John."

Shore was implying Sicilians were capable of such irrational, hot-blooded action, which had some validity, although Vincent wouldn't admit as much.

"But I'm completely taken aback by this hostile takeover that's been launched. It's as if the entire world has gone mad...or at least our part of it."

"I agree," Vincent said.

"Listen, Vincent, I just got off the phone with Attorney General Travaine. He is, or rather was, a very close friend of Van Epps. They went to Harvard Law together and both started their careers at Black & Lace."

"Yes, I'm aware of that," Vincent interjected.

Shore continued, "Well, Travaine is sending over an Assistant Attorney General to interface with us."

"Leonard, she just left our office."

"Really. Amazing. That was quick. Well, anyway, she works directly for Travaine and his office and can be of great assistance to us. After all, we are one of the few Big Board-listed companies that actually is a New York corporation, not Delaware, and right now, we need all the help we can get. Now, here's what I plan to do: first, I'm sending an e-mail blast to all employees as to what we know, which isn't much at this point, but I will certainly acknowledge the tremendous contributions of the three officers, just as we did with Esposito last week, and DuBois before that, as well as the tragedy of their deaths. The communication will be handled by Spencer, our outside consultant, and will also acknowledge the tender offer that's been launched. The release will state that our Board will evaluate the proposal and comment when appropriate. By the way, I assume you know The Exchange has suspended trading of our stock in light of these shocking events?"

"No, I didn't know that, but that's entirely to be expected."

"Yes, of course," Shore said and continued, "I've also spoken to Tom Gillis at Black & Lace. They will review any press releases, as well as the e-mail of which I spoke. They're gearing up to advise The Board, which by the way, will hold an emergency meeting Monday morning at 9 AM. I expect you to attend the meeting, Vincent."

"Of course," Vincent replied, caught a bit off guard that the Vice Chairman would want him there since he was just

Associate General Counsel for Sterling and had never attended Board meetings in the past.

"In addition, I'd like you to coordinate with Krill Associates to help us with some quick investigative work as to whom the hell the Abba Corporation is and who's really behind this tender. As you may know, Justin Krill was a dear, dear friend of our Chairman. I've also spoken to Justin, and he will personally lead a team of his best agents to assist us. Call him after we conclude."

"Yes, sir."

"Finally, Vincent, I want you to liaison with the law enforcement authorities on this – both the FAA as well as the local police. Find out what they are saying as well regarding this ghastly business with Esposito. I don't want The Board to be surprised by the police findings. The news will be embarrassing and detrimental to us, no matter what it is. The best avenue there is to let the Attorney General's Office lead the way —"

"I'm having dinner with Ms. Dominica tonight," Vincent said, totally agreeing with the Vice Chairman. "We'll be able to go over approaches to all this then."

"Fine, as long as you keep focused on the task at hand."

By now, there was real emotion in Shore's voice, and Vincent not only heard it but sensed the depth of his feelings and concerns.

After all, Travaine was extremely close to David Van Epps as was Krill to Chairman Carradine. It seemed as if they were all connected somehow way beyond Sterling Works. What a tragedy…all these deaths and a bloody takeover to boot.

"Rest assured, Mr. Shore, I know what I need to do."

"Go to it then," Shore replied. "I will call you tomorrow morning about 10 on your cell. I have the number. You can update me then."

Shore lingered on the call a good ten seconds more, then said in a most heavy voice, "Vincent, you are the most senior lawyer in the company now. These are unprecedented times for all of us. Even the most experienced hand would have enormous difficulty managing this crisis, and you are assuming a lead role. Are you up to it?"

"Most definitely, Sir," Vincent replied in a strong voice, without hesitation. "I assure you I will do everything in my power to deal with all of this."

"God help us all, Vincent."

Vincent replaced the receiver with a heavy heart.

The moment the conversation concluded, the formidable Ms. Dudley appeared in his office once more and snapped, "I will get Justin Krill on the line, and while you're talking with him, I'll cancel this dinner tonight with Miss Dominica."

Vincent realized that the old hag had been eavesdropping on his conversation with the Vice Chairman. *What a bitch. And now, she's giving me orders.* Vincent's temper ignited, but somehow, he managed to hold it in check.

In a loud, commanding but even voice, he said, "Thank you, Ms. Dudley, but I prefer to place my own call to Mr. Krill."

That bitch can't listen in on my cell phone, he thought.

"And one other thing…there will be no dinner cancellation. Mr. Shore, as you know, was quite clear about utilizing any, and all, help from the Attorney General's Office. In fact, you can go back to your own office now. I won't need YOUR assistance any further, and please, on your way out, do ask my secretary to step in." With the most pleasant expression on his face that he could muster he added, "Again, thank you, Miss Dudley." And with that, he turned his back on her.

For a second, judging by the lightning he felt striking his back, he thought she was going to take him on, but apparently, she thought better of it and left without saying another word. However, she apparently forgot to send in his secretary.

Vincent smiled at Dudley's classic passive-aggressive behavior and poked his head out of his office. "Marsha, could you join me, please?"

Marsha McGrath had worked for Vincent for several years. She was a Brooklyn girl, married with no children, and had a husband in the Marine Corps deployed to Afghanistan. She was competent, efficient, street smart and extremely loyal to Vincent. She also despised Katherine Dudley and immediately smiled when Vincent deftly banished Dudley from his office.

Marsha came into his office and smoothly closed the door, remaining standing.

"Marsha, I need your help," Vincent said, "and please sit down. I don't have to spell it out for you – we're in a helluva crisis. Frankly, I don't have a clue what's going on, but I've got to get some answers and fast."

Marsha nodded. She was a quick study. Sweet, but Brooklyn-tough. She had already checked her earlier emotions and was ready to charge through a wall for The Sterling Works and for Vincent.

"Vincent, what do you want me to do?" She asked.

"First, get me every scrap of information that's publicly available on the plane crash and the Esposito deaths. Second, call Tom Gillis at Black & Lace. Ask him to e-mail the applicable SEC rules and regs, including Schedule 13D requirements regarding hostile takeovers. Also, have him send any immediate recommendations regarding this particular tender offer. Third, I'm going to be on my cell with Justin Krill in a moment, so don't allow anyone or other phone calls to interrupt. Last, Google Angela Dominica of the N.Y. Attorney General's Office and print out any biographical information on her. I will be having dinner with her later this evening, and I want to know who I'm meeting with."

Vincent paused for a breath and then looked at his secretary. "I tell you again, Marsha, I don't know why or how any of these terrible things are happening, but I know for sure that if this takeover is successful, this great old company and many of our long-time employees, including you and me, will be history. And one more thing regarding the takeover stuff...do your own search on hostile bids. Identify recent ones that were unsuccessful and why they failed. I'm generally familiar with the requirements, but I need to become an overnight expert. Pull as much as can be had in as short a time as possible. Include any helpful articles or summaries. Needless to say, I know, Marsha, but anything you see, hear or touch with regard to all of this is highly confidential."

"Vincent, please, you don't have to worry about me. I know the drill."

"I know you do, but this is the highest level of confidentiality, which means you don't share anything with anyone, no matter how senior, unless I clear it. That includes Master Sergeant Dudley, no matter what she says to you."

Marsha smiled at that directive.

"Oh, and, make a reservation for two at Il Mulino for 9 PM this evening. Be sure to use their special number, otherwise you won't get through until next week. And lastly, call my fraternity brothers at this number, explain what has happened and give them my regrets for this weekend."

"Got it, Vincent. Anything else?"

"Not this second. I'm going to call Justin Krill now, so please guard the door."

Marsha nodded and retreated to her position.

Vincent reached Krill in just a few seconds – clearly Shore had greased the way. They talked for about ten minutes. Justin already had the massive Krill organization in motion. If anyone could get through a corporate shroud of secrecy, it was the Krill people; not only did they have massive data bases of information, but also their international contacts and relationships were the envy of intelligence agencies around the globe.

When Vincent hung up, he hesitated before making a second call, but then quietly dialed his burner phone from memory. He kept this type of phone solely for situations when he wanted no record. There was no number for this contact in any phone directory.

The phone rang four times before it was picked up.

"Yea?" A deep, heavily-accented Italian voice answered.

"This is Vinnie Marcantonio. Ask him if he can meet me at 8:30 tonight."

"Where?"

"The place," Vincent replied.

The phone went dead. Vincent looked at his Cartier. Four hours ago, he was on his way to Boston, a happy guy with few real worries in the world. How could everything wash away in such a short time?

With that one brief concession to self-pity, Vincent steeled himself. Despite everything that had happened, he was now in control of his emotions, and he was thinking clearly, very clearly.

Perhaps there is something deep inside each of us which permits this to happen, a sort of defense mechanism for survival. In any event, he was no longer a shaken shadow of himself, gasping for air in the garage. He had his game face on, and his head was screwed on quite tight.

At that exact moment, The Ghost appeared again.

Vincent froze. "What the hell?!"

The Ghost gripped a volume of Sir Arthur Conan Doyle's classic *Sherlock Holmes* which was on a small table by Vincent's mahogany desk. Vincent loved the supersleuth's tales. His eyes were drawn to the page marked by The Ghost. It was where Holmes tells Watson:

"When you have eliminated the impossible, whatever remains, however improbable, must be truth."

When Vincent looked up from the book, the apparition was gone. *Did I imagine this?* No, he was certain he did not. It was the New York Stock Exchange all over again, except it was today, and this was really happening again. That ghost was trying to tell him something. But what?

The buzzing of his phone interrupted his thoughts. Slowly, he picked up the receiver.

"Vincent, Tom is on the line. He has approved the draft of Shore's e-mail blast and wants your okay before he lets it go. He says you need to turn on your computer. Your copy is there, and he'd like a sign-off in the next sixty seconds," Marsha said.

Vincent was still shaken by The Ghost but managed a firm yes and proceeded to open his email. Shore's message began: "In a bizarre coincidence, two enormous tragedies have occurred today, and I'm deeply saddened to report..."

Two minutes later, the message was out to everyone in the company. However, all Vincent continued thinking about was The Ghost. He looked at the Sherlock Holmes' passage again and then at Shore's words in the email.

Suddenly, it hit him hard – but he'd been thinking it all along...

All these horrible events of the past few days and now the multiple tragedies today, along with the tender offer for The Sterling Works. Coincidences? Esposito's wife murders him and kills herself. The company plane goes down, killing the Chairman, CEO and COO. Frank Dubois, their CFO, is randomly murdered outside a bar. And, while they're all reeling from these occurrences, a hostile takeover is launched.

What if these weren't coincidences? Everyone, including Vincent himself, kept saying that none of this made any sense! Shore's message called it a terrible coincidence of tragic events. But that's not what The Ghost was showing him. Holmes told Watson that if something doesn't make sense, and you ruled out the impossible, then look for the improbable explanation.

Vincent checked his watch and quickly rose from his chair. He whisked past Marsha, but then turned back to her, saying, "Go home soon and get some rest, and call my cell if anyone is trying to reach me, but don't give out my number."

Vincent needed counsel, now more than ever, and it wasn't a lawyer, investigator or anyone like that who could help him.

God, he hoped the message had gotten through. It had been two years since they last spoke. What if he didn't want to see him? What if he would see him but couldn't tonight? *Screw the negative thoughts. He'll be there. He's got to be.* Vincent needed his advice and support more than anything.

Anthony had always had the rare gift of insight, of seeing things the way they really are, rather than the way we want them to be. He knew Vincent wouldn't be calling him unless it was super important.

Chapter 12

Thursday Evening, April 26, 2012
Patsy's Bar & Grille, New York City

Vincent hopped a taxi in front of his building and directed the driver to an address on Mulberry Street in Little Italy, as the area was known. When the cab pulled in front of the unremarkable building, Vincent tossed three fives at the driver, thanked him and jumped out, knowing better than to dawdle.

The two lookouts, which Vincent immediately spotted, were surveying their surroundings. And they weren't standing together, making it much harder to take them out simultaneously. If that was anyone's objective, the two soldiers standing in front of Patsy's Bar & Grille were going to make an attack very difficult, especially since another soldier, who Vincent did not see, was on top of the restaurant roof with a sniper rifle and communicator on his head.

Vincent looked across the street. There was yet another, large, tough-looking man with a cell phone to his ear and a noticeable bulge under his jacket.

He got my message, Vincent realized. *Thank God.*

Vincent entered the bar which had an unusual L-shaped entrance, constructed so that only one person at a time could enter and then only slowly. There were no windows in the entire place.

Inside, there were two barkeeps, acutely eyeing the entrance. The nearest one watched Vincent extremely closely as he tried to adjust his eyes to the dark interior. The second bartender looked at him and smiled.

"Hey, Vinnie M, what the fuck? Haven't seen your face around here for a long time."

Vincent's only reply was a slight nod of his head. Slowly, he walked the length of the bar and took a seat in the second to last booth facing the back door. The booth was constructed of solid steel with a classic saloon wood veneer. Vincent also knew that there was a specially-rigged trap door in the floor of the booth, which when triggered, allowed the person sitting opposite him to escape in a matter of seconds.

There were no other customers in the place and none would be permitted to enter.

Vincent sat very still. He looked at his watch again. It was 8:18 PM – twelve minutes to see if he'd show. Vincent already knew the answer. Of course, he was coming, that's why the place was empty, and the watchers were out front.

Without warning, the back door opened and in walked 250 pounds of massive muscle, followed by a second, somewhat smaller guy, carrying a very high-tech detector box.

"Stand up and empty your pockets...of everything. Place your cell phone and any other similar shit on the table. Take off your coat and hand it to me with your left hand," growled the Fullback.

Vincent did exactly as he was told, mentally noting it was just like Anthony to be early – either that or late – but never when he was expected and never by a familiar routine. One of the many reasons Anthony "One Shot" Vacarro was a walking, breathing, free man while so many of his Italian peers were not.

Vincent noticed that the first bartender now had a pump action 12 gauge shot gun on the bar, pointed directly at him.

A wand was produced, and he was scanned as he stood in the aisle. Then the device was pointed under and around the booth. No listening devices or any other gadgets registered. Vincent's phone went into a steel box, which mysteriously appeared from nowhere.

The Muscle took up station, standing halfway down the aisle facing the front door. Undoubtedly, there were other guards behind the rear door. He spoke something into a handheld communicator but continued to face Vincent, who was told to take a seat in the booth.

Five long minutes passed. Not a word was uttered.

Then the back door opened and in walked Anthony Vacarro, 1st Capo of the largest and most-feared of all the New York five mafia families. Anthony was neither head nor underboss of his family. He was, however, the biggest "producer" of all the crime syndicates and mafia organizations in New York, and undoubtedly the entire country, and his crew was the largest of them all.

Vincent Mark and Anthony Vacarro had grown up together. They were childhood buddies through high school and even while Vincent was at Bowdoin College and Syracuse Law School. Only after that did they drift apart. The two had not seen each other or spoken for over two years.

Anthony was about 5'10" and solid as a rock. He religiously spent two hours a day, every single day of his life, in the gym and followed a very strict diet. As a result, he was in excellent physical condition. He also was always impeccably dressed.

He looked Vincent square in the eyes. "So, Vinnie, I don't hear from you for two years. Two fucking years! You must be in some deep shit. What do you want?"

Vincent froze. He wondered whether he had done the right thing by calling Anthony and coming here to see him. He had been trying to leave this part of his life behind him. *What was he thinking?* He met his old friend's eyes and understood his hurt and confusion.

"Anthony," he stammered, "I don't know where to begin, I —"

Anthony cut him off.

"Vincent, why don't you just tell me what your problem is. Let's not bullshit around. But let me first ask you this…is this about all the shit with your company? Your guy getting wacked in New Rochelle, the plane going down today and that shit with Esposito out on Staten Island? And before you answer, are you aware that you were followed here, that there are two Pros out there waiting for you?"

Vincent was stunned. "Followed? I don't understand, Anthony. What do you mean followed? Why would anyone follow me?" All this came out in a single stream of consciousness.

Anthony looked at him kind of sideways. "You know, Vinnie, sometimes, for a smart guy, you're pretty fucking dumb. Two guys are tailing you, and they're not cops, I can tell you that. They're Pros – no question. Now talk! I've got to make a living, you know."

With that, Vinnie recounted the recent events and ended where he began – Why were these men following him?

Anthony Vacarro listened intently. He didn't interrupt. He didn't ask questions. Most importantly, he didn't hit

Vincent in the head with his sledgehammer of a fist, although he had several impulses to do just that.

When Vincent concluded, Anthony asked him one question. "What is it you want from me?"

Vincent took a deep breath, maybe the longest and deepest breath he had drawn in the two years they hadn't spoken. "I need your help, Anthony. I need to know what really happened to Frank Dubois in New Rochelle, what really took place with the Espositos in Staten Island and with The Sterling Works' plane crash this morning. And last, I need to know why am I being followed."

Anthony looked hard at his childhood buddy. Vincent Marcantonio had saved his life when they were both eighteen. They had since gone their separate ways, with Vincent entering Bowdoin College then Syracuse Law School and Anthony enlisting in the United States Marine Corps followed shortly after his discharge by initiation into La Cosa Nostra. Up until two years ago, they had always stayed in touch. Neither of them had ventured into the other's world, however. Then shortly after his mother's death, Vincent cut off contact with his old buddy. Not many things got through Anthony Vacarro's tough hide, but this loss of contact materially affected him.

"Alright, Vinnie, I'll help you, but don't expect me to buy this Vincent Mark bullshit. You're Vinnie Marcantonio, whether or not you forget the old neighborhood and continue running away from your own name. I know who you are, even if you don't. First thing I'll tell you is I'm fifty-fifty sure the guys outside are there to take you out. And I'm one hundred percent sure they want to know what you're doing. Second, you have to be a fucking idiot not to see that everything that's been happening is because somebody wants your fucking company. No ifs, ands or buts. They want your company!"

"But why, Anthony? I mean Sterling Works is a public company, but we're not a high flyer with some huge valuation. Why would anyone wage a massive killing spree for The Sterling Works?"

Vacarro looked at him sideways once again and said, "Fuck, Vinnie, it's about MONEY! It's always about money. Didn't they teach anything useful in all those fucking schools you went to? It always comes down to the fucking money. You may not see it right now, but it's there – I fucking guarantee it."

Vincent thought about his encounters with The Ghost – maybe that's what it was trying to communicate.

Vacarro continued, "Listen to me, Vinnie, you figure out where the hidden prize is buried in that fucking company of yours, and then things that don't make sense now, will make perfect sense. Get it?"

Vincent did get it. He just didn't know where it would lead him. "Yea, alright Tony, I see what you are saying, but —"

"No fucking buts!" Vacarro half exploded. "Man, I hate that yes-but-shit!" He lowered his voice. "I'll see what I can find out about the Dubois and Esposito killings. I don't go near anything dealing with the Feds, including the FAA. Your legal eagles can track that shit down, but I'll will find out who these guys outside are. In the meantime, Vinnie, make damn sure they don't put you down. *Capisce*? And give me your cell number. I'll call you in a couple days and let you know when we can talk again. It won't be here."

Vincent understood. Anthony Vacarro was a gangster, but he was a very careful one. He moved around and constantly varied his daily patterns. Vincent would get a call to meet only minutes before Anthony would see him.

"Anthony, you ought to know that the Attorney General's Office sent a woman lawyer over this afternoon to help me and The Sterling Works. I'm having dinner with her in fifteen minutes at Il Mulino."

Vacarro stood up. "I don't care who you have dinner with as long as the conversation isn't about me. I'll tell you this though, Vinnie, whatever you do, don't screw around with prosecutors. It always turns out badly. And, Vinnie, I'm not just talking about deals." He looked his old friend straight in the eye. "And one last thing, Vinnie…try to keep from getting your skinny ass shot off. I don't have time to go to your fucking funeral."

Anthony gave his old buddy a bear hug and disappeared through the back door with his crew. Vincent's phone was returned to him. The shotgun had disappeared as silently as it initially appeared. The tall guy at the entrance told him in perfect Italian that it was okay to go outside now. He, too, retreated then through the back entrance.

The two men in front of Patsy's and the third watcher across the street were nowhere to be seen. It was just as if the meeting had never taken place. Vincent hailed a taxi, jumped in and told the driver the address for Il Mulino. The cabbie already knew it well.

Vincent had seven minutes to make it on time. Not bloody likely in New York traffic. I wonder if they're tailing me now, he thought, fighting the urge to look out the back window.

Chapter 13

Vincent arrived at 86 W 3rd Street at 9:20 – twenty minutes late. The maître d' told him that his lady guest was already seated, and, he added in a conspiratorial whisper, "She's quite a beauty, Signore Mark. Good luck!"

Vincent went to their table and extended his hand and apologies, "I'm so sorry, Ms. Dominica. I ran late with my last meeting and couldn't break away. I hope you'll forgive me."

"It's certainly not a problem, Mr. Mark, and quite understandable, given what you are dealing with." Her smile lit up the room. "By the way, can we drop the formalities? My name is Angela."

"And mine is Vincent," he replied in kind.

They each ordered a glass of Montepulciano red wine while the unparalleled Il Mulino waiter showered them with imported Parmigiano-Reggiano cheese from Calabria, and other assorted, delicious Italian foodstuff.

Vincent thought Angela was absolutely stunning, with such grace. A very classy lady.

At the same time, Anthony Vacarro's words rung loudly in his ears, "Don't screw around with prosecutors, Vincent, it always turns out badly."

Like most men his age, Vincent promptly deposited his friend's sound advice in his mental waste basket while he allowed his virile libido to take over.

"Well, Angela, where do we begin? I suppose I ought to tell you who I am and what I do at The Sterling Works."

"Not necessary, Vincent," she smoothly replied. "I know a great deal about you, including that you changed your name. Why may I ask?"

Somewhat taken aback, Vincent replied, "My given name is Marcantonio. It's way too long and too ethnic to be used in business, so I shortened it to Mark. That's four letters and very easy to remember. In fact, that's one characteristic people always seem to recall about me."

"Hmmm, well, forgive me, but I doubt the real reason is anything as simple as that," she said. "However, I also know that you graduated from Bowdoin College in Brunswick, Maine. Interestingly, so did I."

"You're kidding," Vincent said and laughed.

"No, I am Class of 2009."

"That explains it partly then. I was a Senior when you were a Freshman, although I can't believe I didn't notice a first-year student as charming as you."

"You're very kind." Angela smiled graciously then switched to her all-business posture. "Let's allow the waiter to order for us. We have a lot to discuss and not a lot of time."

"Good idea," Vincent conceded, somewhat reluctantly.

Angela Dominica, Assistant Attorney General for New York State, took a sip of her wine, squared her shoulders and literally leaned in. "Vincent, it wasn't chance that the

AG assigned me to liaison with your company. In truth, I requested it."

"Oh," Vincent said, most intrigued to hear more, "and why was that?"

"Because, Vincent, like you, I had an encounter with The Ghost of Bowdoin College." She paused, letting this information sink in. As soon as she saw that her startling revelation had registered, she continued, "Vincent, I know that you also had an experience with The Ghost. I'll tell you how I know later, but the important thing is, this was my second time. It happened after the supposed mugging death of your CFO, Frank Dubois. The Ghost appeared to me in my apartment and pointed to the article which appeared in the New York Post."

"I remember the headlines," Vincent chimed in, "Finance Exec loses Baume & Mercier and Life."

"Yes, well, The Ghost made it very clear to me that it wasn't a mugging."

"How?" Vincent asked, still totally surprised by the turn their conversation had taken.

"It doesn't matter right now," Angela said hurriedly, "but what does matter is that I believe all these recent events concerning The Sterling Works are connected."

Vincent thought about his meeting with Vacarro less than an hour earlier. Anthony was just as emphatic about a connection, and, at least, he didn't base his opinion on some ridiculous ghostly spirit.

"Now, Angela —"

"Hold on, Vincent," she said firmly, "let me finish. As I said, this is not my first encounter with The Ghost. The first time happened during my senior year at Bowdoin. My roommate, who had broken up with her longtime boyfriend, along with two other girls, were going to drive down to UNH and celebrate her new freedom. She pleaded with me to go with them that afternoon. I decided not to. And yes, I had exams coming up to study for, but the real reason I didn't go was that I had a spooky experience in my room earlier that day. The Ghost appeared to me and made it very clear that something bad was going to happen. I pleaded with my roommate not to drive down there, told her what had happened to me, but she just laughed and said I must be studying too hard and hallucinating. Anyhow, the three girls left that afternoon, partied until 2 AM and then started back to Bowdoin while blind drunk. They went off Route 1 in York, Maine at over 100 mph. All three were killed. If I had gone with them that afternoon, I, too, would have died that night."

"Yes," Vincent said, feeling an all-too-familiar unsettling in his stomach with her accounting of her supernatural experience, "I remember reading about that accident. It was incredibly tragic. My God, Angela, do you really believe your experience actually involved a ghost?"

"Yes, absolutely, Vincent, and it wasn't just some ghost, it was The Ghost of Bowdoin College. Surely, you know about all the legends and stories."

"Yes, of course, I do. Everyone who goes to Bowdoin has heard about The Ghost, but how does the situation at The Sterling Works tie in with that old legend?"

Angela Dominica stiffened. "Vincent, don't be coy with me. You told a number of people about what happened to you in 2009 and how an apparition led you away from that gunman."

Vincent's face softened. "Yes, that's true. Although, I will tell you that, as months and years have passed, I'm less and less certain about what happened that day. In fact, Angela, it all seems kind of a blur now, except for one thing, which I shouldn't tell you but —"

Angela finished his sentence for him, "...The Ghost visited you again didn't he, Vincent...and recently? So, when did he appear and what happened?"

Fortunately for Vincent, their entrees arrived, which gave him a chance to assimilate everything Angela had said, and more significantly, time to decide how much he was going to share with her. Part of him wanted to pull back, preferring a conservative approach before he opened up all the way; on the other hand, she was strikingly beautiful and something about her excited him and made him want to tell her everything he was thinking and feeling.

Once again, Anthony's words of caution echoed in his head, but as young men often do, Vincent chose to take the advice of his other head.

"Listen to us, Angela," he said, "we're talking about ghosts and spirits like a couple of high school kids."

"No, Vincent, we're not. You and I have both had real, not imagined experiences and our lives were dramatically affected, both, thank God, for the better."

"Granted, something strange happened to me back in 2009, but at this point, Angela, I'm not exactly sure what took place. As I said, it all started to blur."

"Sure, it did, Vincent, except for one thing...The Ghost appeared again. And recently, didn't it?"

Reluctantly, Vincent admitted that, indeed, The Ghost had appeared to him less than two hours ago, and he relayed the scene with the Sherlock Holmes' passage.

Angela's eyes were on fire. She was animated beyond description. "I knew it, Vincent! I knew that something was very wrong with all this! The Ghost was trying to tell you that things are not what they seem. That's what the passage is saying. When something doesn't make sense, you have to keep digging. When you eliminate the impossible, whatever is left, no matter how improbable, must be the truth. And that's where we are right now."

She took another bite of her pasta. "This is incredibly delicious, by the way! Il Mulino is simply the best!"

Vincent nodded, wondering to himself how this woman could be talking about ghosts one minute and raving about food the next. *Women...they're very complex, and I don't think I will ever truly understand them, which, of course, is perfectly true for all mankind, right?*

"Look, Vincent, I've been drawn to this whole ghost business ever since that fateful weekend with my roommate at Bowdoin. I wouldn't be here with you right now in Il Mulino if it wasn't for The Ghost. I think it's real. I don't know how or why, but somehow, I've been brought into this situation with your company. After the New York Post article, I went to the Attorney General, who, frankly, likes me because of some work I did directly for him. I asked him if our office should be investigating. At that point, he said there wasn't anything to investigate, but after today's events, he called me in and explained how your COO and he were old law school buddies and were very close. He's devastated by the death of his friend. He said I should contact The Sterling Works and offer any help our office can properly provide. When I checked the roster of management, I saw your name and that you had gone to Bowdoin. With the help of Google and a few phone calls, I learned about you and the story of what happened at the NYSE. I knew you were the one to see, and now...here we are."

Vincent found himself even more attracted to this woman, if that were even possible. "Ok...I won't quibble over what you've said, but let me ask you this, if a ghost exists, how does he know what's going to happen before it happens? Why does he appear to you and me but not to someone else? For example, wouldn't it be better if he appeared before your boss, the Attorney General? If he was convinced by this thing, he is someone who could really wield power."

All the while he spoke, another part of Vincent's brain was still replaying his meeting with Vacarro and his old friend's warning to guard against any attraction to a law enforcement person.

Angela completed another mouthful of pasta.

Lord, the girl can eat, Vincent thought, amazed and impressed.

Despite the increasing noise in the incredibly busy restaurant, Angela calmly and clearly replied. "I don't have all the answers to your questions, but I'm convinced I need to return to Bowdoin College and see if I can find some answers there, at least as it pertains to The Ghost. If we can get some insight as to this ghostly business, I believe it will help us unravel the sordid Sterling Works' situation. Maybe we can solve the mystery of these deaths and save your company. I also realize that you have a lot of things to do now, especially with this tender offer looming. There's got to be a lot of legal work going on and Board activities, all without the benefit of Sterling Works' top leadership."

"You're right, of course," Vincent agreed, even though he was a bit disappointed she evidently didn't include him in the top leadership circle. "I'll be up to my proverbial neck in legal stuff. Speaking of which, that brings me to something your office can supply. Any kind of support in the form of an affidavit from the AG's Office concerning the New York anti-takeover statute would be extremely helpful, as well as much-appreciated."

"Yes, of course," she answered, nodding her head as if it were a done deal. "I know just what you need. I had an associate assigned to me start working on such an affidavit before I went to your office. He'll get it cranked out, and I'll have a draft over to you this weekend. Here's my card with both my cell phone and e-mail address." Barely pausing to breathe, she continued, "I've decided to drive up to Brunswick tomorrow morning."

"What?!" Vincent shouted, forgetting they were in a restaurant, immediately feeling bad he'd lost his cool, despite realizing the noise of the crowd probably buried the better part of his outburst.

Still, a few patrons near their table looked over at them, probably trying to decide whether or not Angela was in danger. Angela got up and made nice with them to erase their concerns.

While she was at their table, Vincent couldn't help but sneak a peek at her gorgeous legs.

Men are just so predictable.

When she returned, Vincent lowered his voice and said, almost whispering, "What can you do up there?"

"Look, Vincent," she leaned in, matching his near-whisper, "The Ghost is from Bowdoin. It all started there. If I can find out how, who, why and so on, I think it will help me immensely in understanding its involvement in your company. Don't worry, as I said, I have what you need already in the works regarding the affidavit. I will have it cleared with the AG and will email it to you from Bowdoin for your review. By the way, give me your business card with your cell phone and email address, please. I don't know what I'll learn in Brunswick, but that's where it all began, and so I feel certain that is where I need to be."

Vincent felt the start of a dull ache in his head. Maybe it was the wine or maybe it was overload. Too much happening too fast. Plane crashes. Multiple deaths. Reconnecting with Anthony. His warning. This woman.

Displaced spirits. As he mentally went through the list, the ache grew sharper.

"Angela, I'm sorry I reacted that way," he said and sighed. "It's just that with everything going on, I'm wound pretty tight right now. Honestly, I thought you would be able to help me during these intense, next few days. Frankly, with all due respect, I'd much rather have you counseling me on how to handle this takeover attack than chasing ghost stories up in Maine. I mean, you don't really believe this stuff, do you?"

Angela Dominica looked Vincent straight in the eye with an icy glare. She said slowly, with an absolute, iron firmness, "Vincent, I do believe that there is a spirit at work here. I've experienced it, and so have you. Apparently, others at Bowdoin have had encounters as well. My life was forever changed because of The Ghost. So was yours. The Ghost has returned, and there's a reason. You are in great danger. My instincts are screaming that these deaths around you are not coincidental, and they are not accidental. I AM going to help you. And I believe that the very best assistance I can provide you is to get to the bottom of this ghost business. As I already said, I have someone at the office working on the State's affidavit to support The Sterling Works. I'm sure your attorneys are going to ask for a restraining order, preventing the tender offer from going forward, at least temporarily. The affidavit from the New York Attorney General's Office will certainly help."

She smiled, and it was the warmest, most beautiful smile Vincent had ever been on the receiving end of in his life (except for his mother, of course).

"May I again suggest that you give me your business card with cell and email information, and that we finish this delicious dinner along with Il Mulino's excellent merlot."

Vincent felt his mouth drop wide open. Never, in his life, had he ever experienced a woman like the one sitting across from him. And, to be honest, he wasn't quite sure what to do with her.

"Now, Vincent, why don't you tell me why you changed your name to Mark from Marcantonio, which I personally think is simply a splendid Italian name, both musical as well as informative," she said, changing gears, sweetly and cleverly changing the subject as if she were in these kinds of situations all the time.

With that, she gracefully placed another bite of her scrumptious ravioli between her exquisite, ruby red lips and swallowed. Vincent had great difficulty not choking as he struggled to answer her pointed question.

"That's a fair question, but it's sort of hard to explain."

She said nothing, waiting on him to enlighten her with his explanation.

"You see, I came from a rough Italian neighborhood. I had no brothers or sisters. Which made me —"

"It makes you an only child," she said, finishing his sentence as well as correcting the tense.

"Yes. And a few years ago, my mother died. My father passed away some time ago. I was, in some ways, trying to leave a difficult past behind me."

Angela frowned, letting Vincent know by her expression alone that he was going to have to be much more direct and get to the real reason.

"I grew up with Anthony Vacarro. He was my best friend. Really, he was the brother I never had. Do you know who he is?"

Without hesitating at all, she said, "Vincent, everyone in New York City knows who Anthony Vacarro is. Of course, I know who he is, but what's your point?"

"Well, we were extremely close through high school and even after that. But we were going in different directions. He's part of a different world. I went to law school. I wanted to practice corporate law for a large company. Many of the people I deal with went to prep schools and Ivy League colleges and universities. I'm a public-school boy. I ran with a very different crowd. My childhood best friend is now the Captain of the biggest mafia crew in New York City."

"So that's why you changed your name?" Angela asked with a challenge in her tone. "You thought you could become less Italian, more acceptable, if there wasn't a vowel at the end of your name? Sounds like an identity crisis to me, Vincent."

An identity crisis? Vincent suddenly thought about something else Anthony had said: "Vincent, you don't even know who you are anymore." *Wasn't that a line in someone's play or was it a Seinfeld episode? Either way, no good.*

"No, Angela, I wouldn't call it an identity thing. I know who I am. I —"

Angela again interrupted. "Do you now? Well, Vincent, who are you then?"

Before he could answer, she pushed away her dish and said, "It isn't important what I think about this, Vincent, but it is very important what you think and whether you are being honest with yourself. I'll tell you, in no uncertain terms, I am very proud of my Italian heritage. I'm proud of the accomplishments of Italian Americans. I've spent considerable time studying our heritage, our culture, history and all that goes with it. I love the fact that I can speak Italian with a good accent and that I can be understood in our ancestral language, the language of Dante. I love Roma, Firenze and Venezia. We, you, in particular, have a lot of important things to do right now, but at some future point, I would like to discuss this more with you. Okay? In short, Vincent, I'm not buying that you needed a shorter name to advance your career."

Vincent was thoroughly relieved with her brief reprieve. He wasn't ready to dive deeper into his name change and where he came from. Anthony's words, as well as Angela's questions, had stung him, and he was already under so much fire from everything else going on. He didn't need an identity crisis at the same time.

"Fair enough. We'll discuss it some other time." Which, of course, meant there would be a future date with this woman who had literally enchanted him, and that was more than fine with him.

As they paid the check, which they split equally, and moved toward the door, Vincent could barely control himself. *This woman is drop dead gorgeous. And those legs...*

Vincent did not know at this moment just how prophetic his words were as far as living or dying. But before he could say anything further to her in front of the restaurant, she stuck out her hand and shook his. With the other arm, she deftly flagged down a taxi.

As she slid across the rear seat, she smiled again at him and said, "I'll call you by 6 tomorrow night. Check your email before then. We will have a draft affidavit for you to review. I'm guessing that you're headed to your luxurious offices now. Good luck, Vincent, and be careful. You and I don't really know what we're dealing with here, but we do know that people have died, and that means we, too, could be in serious danger."

The door slammed shut, and the taxi sped off.

Chapter 14

Vincent felt very alone. Everything was happening so quickly, and he didn't feel like he was in control of any of it, which, in truth, was quite accurate. He looked around the busy streets outside Il Mulino and suddenly felt utterly vulnerable.

What had Anthony said? God, he wished he was here with him now. Why had he turned his back on his old friend these past two years? Wait a minute, he thought, to be fair, the guy's a criminal. He couldn't pal around with a mafia captain, not without a negative stain attaching to him, too. Then, just as quickly, he said to himself, bullshit, a friend is a friend…someone who sticks with you no matter what!

Vincent's head started to pound again. All this was beginning to get to him. It was a little after 10:30 PM. Angela was right. He should stay with The Sterling Works' situation, not worry about The Ghost. He decided to check in with Black & Lace and see if they had any news. The young grunts would be toiling away, probably all night. He took out his phone and called them.

One of Tom Gillis's many assistants answered without Vincent even catching his name. "Vincent, how are you holding up? Why don't you head over here, and I can brief you on where we are and outline what's coming next."

With that, Vincent looked for a taxi but wasn't as fortunate or talented as Angela at securing one. I bet she never has to wait for a taxi, no matter what the weather is, he thought. For a second, he thought about taking the subway. The underground rail is still the absolute fastest way to access anyplace in Manhattan. But something in his brain vetoed the thought.

Anthony said to watch out for his ass, his skinny ass, actually... certainly better than fat ass. Anyhow, Vincent felt way too vulnerable standing around waiting for a taxi, like a sitting duck. With a wee bit of luck on his side, though, one rounded the corner and headed straight for his extended arm. In he popped.

"20 Broad Street, please."

The cab shot off, weaving expertly around double-parked cars and slow-moving vehicles, to say nothing of all the pain-in-the-anterior pedestrians.

Vincent couldn't stop himself; he scanned out through the back window, trying to see if anyone was following him. His phone went off, startling him half out of his seat. No caller id, he noted, as he answered.

"Hello?"

"Vinnie, you were followed."

"What?!" Vincent asked, recognizing Anthony Vacarro's voice, relieved for his call. "I was followed?"

"Yes, that's what I said, and listen to me, Vinnie, they shook the guy I put on them easily. You getting this,

~ 85 ~

Vinnie? You got yourself some Pros on your case. Real Pros."

Vincent didn't like this, at all. Again, he scanned the street and all the cars following his taxi. "Didn't know you were checking on me."

"Yea, and I know where are you are right now, Vincent," Anthony said, "so have yourself completely ready when the cab stops, pay the fare right now, and when the car stops, get out fast and into that building. Don't screw around. Don't look around. And don't stand in one place once you're inside the building. Keep moving. I'll have a couple boys over there in ten minutes. When you come out, my men will be in a black town car, license RDX 114. Get into that car…and fast. They'll take you to your apartment. Lock the door. My guys will cover you tonight."

Then the phone went dead.

Vincent didn't like any of this. But right now, he was damn glad his old friend Anthony was helping him. He didn't want to end up like Esposito or any of the rest of his coworkers. Then he thought of Angela. He pulled out her card and called her cell.

"Yes, Vincent."

She must have identified him from the number on her cell screen. She'd already added him to her contacts. Good to know, he thought.

He explained what was going on.

"Don't worry, Vincent, no one is following me. I'm sure of it. Right now, I couldn't be safer."

She didn't offer details, which Vincent didn't like, but he didn't have time to play games with her, so he urged her to be careful and signed off.

By this point, his cab had reached 20 Broad, so he hurriedly fished a twenty out of his pants for a $12 fare. He literally jumped out of the taxi and raced through the three glass doors in as secure a fashion as he could muster.

Flashing his ID at the security guard, he was relieved his name was already at the desk, pre-cleared. With a building pass in hand, he headed for the second elevator bank and stopped at the high speed smart cab. Within fifteen seconds, he was on the 27th floor.

As he exited the elevator car, there was an administrative assistant waiting for him. For the $900 per hour they were billing Sterling Works, they could afford to work all night.

Wall Street law firms were an institution unto themselves in New York. They evolved from the 1800's in parallel to the growth of big business. By the late 1960's, they had grown to sizes of 100 to 200 attorneys, but in today's environment, they had "supersized" to 1000 or more attorneys per firm. The business model itself, however, had changed very little during all this growth. Essentially, lawyers were a feudal caste system: Partners and Associates, or better put, the aristocracy and the serfs. The latter were little more than literal servants. They ground out the work, keeping meticulous track of their time (note: time is not the same as results) in 6-minute increments. Clients were billed time charges by all the lawyers assigned to each matter, plus, of course, all the incidental expenses, usually with a hefty markup.

Billing rates ranged from a few hundred dollars to over $1000 per hour. The Partners set the rates by adding up all their expenses, then adding a very healthy profit margin. The net result was that every billable hour was profitable because all the expenses of the firm were included in the charges. Thus, the more billable hours, the more profit there was to divide among the Partners.

The serfs, or Associates, received little or no training or mentoring; instead, they were subject to the sink or swim standard. Regardless of how good or bad their work product was, Associates were to bill as much time as possible, at least 2500 hours a year, and, in many cases, well over 3,000 hours. If the Associate's rate was $500 per hour, well...you can do the math. And, remember, the clients pay regardless of whether the lawyer is successful. Since all the firms operate the same way, it's one grand club.

The goal of the Associate is to make Partner. In the "old days," it took about 10 years. But in today's environment, it can happen in 5 to 7 years, so these grunts sacrifice everything in their personal lives to win the Partnership Prize. It's a helluva existence, and not all lawyers aspire to this.

These thoughts raced thru Vincent's mind as he hurried along the hallways full of law factory worker bees, every lawyer, paralegal, technician and others bent over their computers, cranking out who only knows what.

Man, am I glad I opted out of this slave pit, he thought, as he arrived at the office he was told to go to. One of Tom's assistants greeted him warmly, but it wasn't even the one he'd talked to on the phone. Vincent knew because his voice was different. He didn't even bother remembering the names anymore.

"Good to see you, Mr. Mark, though certainly not under these circumstances. Have you heard anything from the FAA about the crash?"

"No, I haven't," Vincent replied.

"Well, the NYPD has no information for us on the Esposito situation, either."

That doesn't sound right, Vincent thought. Double deaths of a man and woman are an unusual situation, even in this city.

"It is a most vexing situation," the assistant said as he offered Vincent a seat and coffee, as if it were 7 in the morning instead of after 10:30 at night. "Well, Mr. Mark, I can assure you, as I'm sure you can tell by the activity here tonight that, we are priming the pumps for this week. As you know, our strategy is to buy time for the Board. That is to say...give the Directors an opportunity to evaluate the proposal and then accept, reject or negotiate better terms. The speed with which this was launched is rather amazing and quite well-coordinated. I must say that their 13D SEC filing, while virtually devoid of any real information, does seem to comply with the regs."

Holy crap! These guys have already thrown in the proverbial towel. Don't they realize their firm will lose an old, respected client that has always paid its bills on time? The thought entered his mind, briefly, as to the possibility this firm had already lined up a future deal with the new boys.

Vincent decided to pose this unlucky messenger a question, "Well then...I'm sorry...what did you say your name was?"

"Dan Howell, sir," the assistant said with not near as much confidence as he had moments before while feeding Vincent the party line.

"Great, Dan...why don't we start with who the hell are these people?! Where are they from? What's their background?"

"Ah...you see...that's where their cleverness really shines through, Mr. Mark. The actual offer is being made by a Delaware Corporation, newly-formed, solely for the purpose of acquiring The Sterling Works' stock. In turn, the Delaware company is owned by a Luxembourg limited liability corporation. Luxembourg is a good country for secrecy, as I'm sure you know. That corporation, in turn, has but one Director, a local lawyer, who is the Director for hundreds of these companies, and they, my friend, are 100% owned by a Caymans Island company, all of whose Officers and Directors are attorneys and Cayman citizens. Under Cayman law, they are not required to disclose anything. They hire themselves out for this very purpose of absolute secrecy and confidentiality. The Caymans' stock, allegedly, according to their Schedule 13D, is owned by a trust, by one man – a Swiss national who is, guess what, a Swiss attorney. The funds then for the all-cash offer for The Sterling Works will come from United Swiss Bank, which has guaranteed the entire credit for the takeover, which amounts to roughly about a billion dollars." And just like that, Dan rebounded, thanks to a well-rehearsed playbook.

"What has Krill dug up on this Swiss guy and all these shell companies?" Vincent asked, more than exasperated by the legal bullshit he just heard.

"Surprisingly, nothing, beyond what I've told you. Of course, it's early, so give Krill a chance."

Vincent was beyond taken aback. "You mean to tell me, the world-renowned Krill Associates' data bases have nothing on any of this?"

"That's exactly what I mean, Mr. Mark, at least at this point. Remember, we've been at this for less than twelve hours."

"I realize that," Vincent replied, knowing damn well that twelve hours was an eternity for firms like Black & Lace and Krill Associates. "But this is all a classic smoke screen. You know that as well as I do. Well…I would certainly hope so, for your sake," Vincent snapped. "The disclosure

~ 90 ~

rules and the SEC were supposed to put an end to this kind of nonsense years ago."

"True, Mr. Mark, true, except that the SEC quit vigorously pursuing enforcement. It ain't what it used to be, as the saying goes. We all know how they fell on their proverbial asses with the Bernie Madoff case, and that's only the tip of the iceberg. However, at this point, for your case, it appears their disclosure requirements are being met."

"Give me a fucking break!" Vincent snarled. "On top of their *noncompliant* disclosure, their so-called premium price is a relative low one, at best."

"Sure, but as you say…it's relative. Your stock, one day before the offer, was trading midway between the low and high price for the preceding twelve months, Mr. Mark, and in this post-recession, sluggish economy, it would hardly be considered predatory, even as an argument."

Vincent was getting more and more frustrated and pissed by the second. "What do you intend to do then? What do you have all these people working on?!"

"Buying you time, Mr. Mark, buying you time. Maybe Krill will come up with something on who is behind this. Maybe they will agree that the other stakeholders, namely employees, suppliers, and the communities you are in, should all be considered, especially when so little is known about the prospective new owners."

"I just don't get it," Vincent said, shaking his head in disgust, but not defeat.

This all reminded him of a scene with Robert DeNiro in the movie *Ronin*. If something doesn't feel right, it isn't. DeNiro avoided getting his head blown off because he listened to his instincts.

Vincent had very strange feelings about everything that was happening. Should he give in to those feelings or analyze everything on a strictly factual basis? He knew the answer he was supposed to choose. Professionally, he had been trained to deal with concrete evidence, not instincts. Yet, every successful lawyer, as well as business leader, would tell you that, at the end of the day, they accomplished their best work when they followed their intuition.

This takeover stinks.

"Ok, Dan, I get the picture, but I want you to dig as deep as you're allowed to, and I expect you to be a pit bull with the Judge on getting these guys to open up and identify the real people behind this. Plus, help Krill anyway you can. That team has never failed before. And I don't want The Sterling Works to be their first strikeout."

"I assure you, again, that we've pulled out all the stops on this one. I'll call you before the Board Meeting on Monday to give you an update as to where we are at that point."

Vincent looked Dan Howell directly in the eyes and said, "Good luck to all of us then. Hell, you don't want to lose a good-paying client, right?"

Howell smiled weakly and replied, "I never enjoy losing a client, a good-paying or otherwise."

With that, Vincent left the room, took the speedy elevator to the lobby, dropped off his security pass and scanned the street for the black town car Anthony had promised him. It was right in front of the building, with his name scrawled on a piece of cardboard in the passenger window.

As the back door swung open, Vincent ran out the entrance of Black & Lace and all but dove into the back seat.

Chapter 15

Friday Evening, April 27, 2012
Brunswick, Maine

It was Friday night and Angela had been driving about four hours. She was exhausted as she checked into the Stowe House, just off the Bowdoin campus. In this very building, Harriet Beecher Stowe had written the pivotal Civil War book *Uncle Tom's Cabin*. Abraham Lincoln himself said, upon meeting Stowe, "so you are the little woman who wrote the book that started this great war."

The aura of all this history enveloped her as she entered the home. Trying to process the events of the past few days, her mind raced. She had become obsessed with the ghost business, leaving her certain of only one thing…she had to get to the bottom of this mystery.

Her instincts, however, screamed danger, and she fought to keep herself calm and under control.

According to the legends she heard while an undergraduate at Bowdoin College, The Ghost's story started when the college was very young, and it involved one of the students. Apparently, so the stories went, from time-to-time, The Ghost would appear to a student or graduate, Robert E. Peary and Joshua Chamberlain being two such examples. And, of course, The Ghost appeared to her, literally saving her life that fateful day. And then there were two admitted occurrences with Vincent Mark.

Angela didn't imagine The Ghost's presence, and she believed Vincent's encounters were real, too, even if he personally wouldn't come to grips with them.

It all began here, she thought. And that's why she had to come here tonight. Somewhere, on this campus, there must be a key to all this.

It occurred to her that the Administration must know something, maybe everything, about their ghost. She wasn't a naturally-gifted detective, but all these incidents could not happen without the Administration, both then and now, digging into them. Of course, no college wants to advertise they have a resident apparition as that certainly would not be good for admissions or rankings.

But, it was too late tonight to dig further. She had to put this stuff out of her mind for at least the rest of the night and get some rest. With that decision made, her pulse slowed to a normal rate. She quietly undressed and collapsed into her bed, hopefully without any ghost-filled dreams.

Sometime in the middle of the night, she bolted upright from a deep slumber, and a bone-deep chill crept through her entire body. Struggling to regain complete consciousness, she felt as if a white cloud had swallowed her whole. As her brain kicked back into gear, the cloud moved away.

Oh my God! It's The Ghost!

Without moving any other muscles, her eyes followed the apparition. It was pointing to the door. The Ghost wants me to open the door, she said to herself. *Why, why would I do that?* And yet, that's exactly what she did, taking each step down the hallway gingerly.

There was absolute silence. Now she was wide awake and experiencing real fear. Fear of what though, she asked herself. Why this sense of impending doom? *This is stupid! Get ahold of yourself.*

Her eyes never left the apparition. It was beckoning her to the end of the hallway, and then it disappeared around the corner. Without knowing why or even how, Angela kept her feet moving in pursuit. I'm crazy, she thought, absolutely nuts.

She moved through the corridor more swiftly now. Her muscles and mind well-focused and perfectly functioning. Just as a second wave of apprehension seized her, she moved around the corner.

Powerful arms seized her then clamped a thick, gloved hand over her mouth. She panicked. She couldn't move, and for several seconds, she couldn't breathe. Don't panic, she tried to convince herself. Yet, she was panicking, like most of us would. Stop panicking, she screamed inside her head.

The bear of a man gripping her spoke, "Listen to me, we're not here to hurt you, we're here to keep you safe. I'm going to remove my hand from your mouth. And whatever you do, don't scream. Listen to me, ok? You got it?"

Angela nodded her head yes. The Bear released his grip and dropped the glove covering her mouth. Angela screamed as loud as she could.

"Oh shit," The Bear said. "You dumb broad, why did you have to scream? Didn't you hear me? We're not your fucking killers. They are!"

As Angela looked down the hall in the direction The Bear was pointing, she saw two, tall and angular, but athletically-built men, both well over six-feet. They had big guns with long barrels pointed at her.

She heard a ping and felt a whish inches from her face. She had only been saved from taking that bullet by The Bear, who pulled her back around the corner in the proverbial nick of time. At the same moment, his partner had a gun drawn and fired. Again, no loud noise, just a ping. Obviously, both guns were silenced, so their deadly bullets could snuff out life without the rest of the world hearing it.

The second set of attackers both froze, dropped to the floor and fired rapidly in unison.

Angela was numb, not able to completely process what was happening. Fortunately, her Italian genes fired, namely the two thousand years of history imbedded in her DNA. Like a Roman soldier from ancient times, her guided response was "fight…not flight."

Her newly-discovered defenders must have sensed the change in her because they moved back quickly to the motel exit door, dragging her with them. They knew and were obviously much more practiced at this than she was, that this was not the time to attack.

The Bear smoothly swung Angela over his shoulders in a soldier's carry. Then he and his partner moved quickly and silently out the door and split in different directions. The partner veered left and The Bear with Angela over his shoulders headed right. Both simultaneously dropped to the ground then and aimed their weapons at the exit.

Angela was near smothering under The Bear, barely able to draw a breath, but completely shielded, nonetheless. Seconds ticked by and nothing happened. There was only silence.

"Johnny," The Bear whispered.

"Yea," the other answered. "I know. They're going to try outflanking us. I'll take it."

Johnny was half The Bear's size but had exceptionally powerful legs. He shot like a rocket from the prone position to a right angle, facing East. The Bear moved Angela and himself to a spot some five-feet-away, facing West.

Angela realized what they had done. They'd executed a field positioning maneuver like well-trained soldiers. The Bear had a cell phone out and speed-dialed even as he continuously scanned the grounds and the door in front of them.

When connected, he said, in a somewhat hushed voice, "Yea, they're here. Two of them. Pros with silenced Sigs, and they are fast as fucking hell. We've got her, though. Alive and safe. For the moment, anyway, but I don't know where they are. Hit the parking lot at the far end, away from the light. You've got three minutes."

He pushed a button on his Tag Heuer chronometer then ended his call.

"Johnny…three minutes. You cover the far end to the left."

"Check" was the reply.

The Bear spoke to Angela without looking at her, shifting his gaze from the field in front of him to what must be their pickup spot.

"Listen, Lady, there are two guys out here trying to kill you…and us because we're in the way. They know what they are doing. We, in turn, are trying to save your ass. To be honest, I'm not sure why we're supposed to protect you, but those are my orders. So…no noisy, dumb ass moves like screaming or running away. Do you understand me?"

Angela nodded her head and meant "yes" this time. She was scared out of her mind and knew only one thing – right now, these two men, whoever the hell they were, were the only thing standing between her and an early grave. Didn't matter why they were here or what they ultimately wanted. It was survival time!

It also occurred to her that The Ghost of Bowdoin College had once again saved her life. If it hadn't woken her up, she'd be a lifeless body in an obscure, historical motel in Brunswick, Maine. Instead, she was alive. Kind of hard to buy it, but this was as real as real gets.

Suddenly, The Bear grabbed her arm. "Listen to me. I'm going to start crawling forward to the parking lot. You keep close but stay to the left of me. If those guys are still here, and they probably are, they'll know we're heading to that lot. So stay close and keep you head down. *Capisce?*"

"*Si, capisco,*" Angela answered in perfect Italian.

"*Buona fortuna ad entrambi*" was the answer she got.

"Yes. Good luck to both of us," she returned his sentiment.

"Head down, remember," The Bear instructed.

Slowly, they made their way. It was cold and damp. It probably had been the entire time they'd been outside the motel, too, but Angela hadn't felt it till now. Her adrenaline was pumping so hard, she hadn't felt anything, but now, her heart rate had slowed a bit, and she was more aware of her surroundings.

This can't be happening, she thought. I don't understand what's going on. At the same time, though, in some far corner of her brain, she did understand. It was connected to The Sterling Works and Vincent Mark.

"Those were not accidents or coincidences," she said out loud. "All those people were murdered."

The Bear looked back and told her to shut up or they would be joining the dead. Angela got it and wrested control of her emotions.

After what seemed like an hour, but was in fact only a minute at most, two things happened in a blur. The Bear grabbed her arm, and a Hummer H3 wheeled into the lot, with no lights, and came to a dead stop. The front door popped open, and the driver was immediately out of the vehicle and behind the left front fender, automatic weapon drawn, sweeping the field. Half running, half being dragged by The Bear, Angela found herself in the front seat, scrunched down, below view. The Bear was prone on the ground, military-style, outside her door.

She heard a low whistle and out of seemingly nowhere, a third partner of The Bear's appeared. In less than thirty seconds, everyone was in the Hummer and they were speeding out of the lot.

Only when they were a quarter mile down the street, did the driver pop on the headlights. And, boy, did Angela have a hundred questions.

Chapter 16

Early Saturday Morning, April 28, 2012
Brunswick, Maine

Of course, she had questions, Vito acknowledged, whether he wanted to or not, and held up his hand. "Wait…I'll answer your questions in about five minutes, after I know they're not following us, which I doubt they will."

Angela closed her mouth, having great difficulty willing herself to wait. She was perspiring heavily and suddenly felt a wave of nausea coming on.

Vito sensed her needs and tapped the driver on his shoulder. "She's going to lose it."

Smoothly, with little effort, as if they'd done this before, the Hummer pulled to the side of the road, the lights went out and the window came down.

Angela felt herself nudged through the opening. She hung over the side and lost it. Gagging, coughing, spitting. She emptied her stomach. It was clearly the after-effect of her near-death experience. Someone handed her a handkerchief. She mumbled "thanks" and cleaned up her face.

"Who were those people?" She asked, gasping for air. "And where are they now?"

Vito answered, "They are professional assassins, and they've been following you. You're supposed to be dead right now. They're gone, for the time being, but they'll pick up our trail soon. I'm Vito. We work for Joey C, who works for Anthony Vacarro. Anthony is an old friend of your friend, Vinnie Marcantonio. Joey told us to track you out of New York and make sure nothing happens to you. Anthony sent three of us, so he must have felt strongly you had a problem. We're quite a ways from our territory. Frankly, I don't like that. I'd like us to head back to the city now, if that's okay with you."

"No, Vito. I'm sorry, but I can't leave now. I don't know what's going on, but I think I can get some answers at Bowdoin College tomorrow, uh, today, since it's now 5 AM."

"Damn," Vito said and shook his head. "I figured you'd say something like that."

Angela took another big gulp of air from the open window, still trying to soothe her wound up system. "I can't thank you enough. Really. You saved my life, and I don't even know your full names."

Vito looked at her and said, "Names don't mean anything, Miss. Orders are what count, and we follow orders real good. We are all Marines, retired from active duty, but always Marines. Our orders are to make sure you're alright, and that's what we've done, at least so far. Now, I really wish you would let us…wait…"

He tapped their driver's shoulder once more. "Headlights are coming up the road behind us, Frankie O."

"Yea, I got it."

With a perfectly executed maneuver, Frankie O did a 180 and was now headed straight at the oncoming sedan.

"Get down now, Miss." Her window was quickly sealed shut.

Vito scanned the car carefully as it passed by, but it was an old guy, alone, who was probably headed to his lobster boat and was late at that.

"Ok. We'll stick with you until I can talk to Joey. I sure as hell ain't calling him at 5 AM, though. That would really piss him off, especially if it wakes up his wife. But you'll do things our way, got it? You'll stay with us in the car until a little after 6. That's when the motel office opens. You can get your stuff from your room, and we'll check your car. Most likely, it's been wired, but we can take care of that. Then, we'll get something to eat and, finally, you can do whatever you came to do. We were told to keep you alive only, not take you anywhere and babysit, so that isn't happening until I talk to Joey."

Angela was feeling a lot better now and some of her conversational skills were returning. "Good. I'm thankful you saved my life and thankful you're not kidnapping me, at least until this Joey says otherwise. You know that I'm Italian, don't you?"

"Yea, I mean, yes, Miss. We know exactly who you are, who your parents are, your job with the State AG, your Audi A6, your birth date and a lot of other things. We guys can Google, just like you. We're only half as stupid as the movies make us out to be. By the way, your grandfather came from Villa San Giovanni in Reggio di Calabria."

"Yes. That's all true, but why are you doing all this for me?" Angela asked politely but firm.

"As I said, we're part of Anthony Vacarro's crew, part of the Family in Manhattan, and you are mixed up in something heavy with Vinnie Marcantonio. Vinnie asked for Vacarro's help, and Anthony figured that you were probably also a target because you've been helping Vinnie.

I don't know how Anthony can anticipate all the stuff he does, but I know he's always right on the money. He sure as hell was right about you."

"Thank you for being honest with me," Angela said.

Vito looked straight into her eyes. "Those guys, the two back there, and I hope that's all there are, they've been tracking you since you left New York City. They're professional killers. They must have a contract on you. Fortunately, it never occurred to them that someone might also be tracking them. We picked them up when you and they crossed into Maine. We already knew where you were headed, so while we were watching out for you, we saw them make their move."

"Shit, Frankie! Hard left! That's them fucking dead ahead now! Move it." Vito said, his hands pressing down on Angela, holding her to the floorboards.

Her heart accelerated with the Hummer.

Frankie executed another perfect 180 and floored the accelerator, to which the Hummer responded. The stock engine had been replaced with a 400 HP special unit, and the vehicle was outfitted with unique, stabilizing bars. They were able to immediately put some distance between the town car and them.

At the same time, Vito was on a phone calling a 9-1-1 Operator. Angela noticed he was using a prepaid, untraceable calling card. "Yes, ma'am. I'm on my way to work and saw two men in a dark black town car acting suspicious right outside Boudreau's gas station on Route 1. They are heading North. They had handguns and were waving them out the window. They scared the hell out of me."

Angela could hear the 9-1-1 operator repeating the information, but Vito clicked off before the operator could ask his name.

The Maine State Police must have had a unit in the immediate area because a patrol car went flying by the Hummer with red lights flashing. In thirty seconds, a local Brunswick police car hit its siren and lights and joined the chase.

"That ought to clear them out...at least for a while. Although, I'm sure the cops will never actually catch them, it will buy us some time. Frankie, head for the motel, the clerk should be up by now."

With all that had happened in the last few minutes alone, Angela had to admire the amazing speed of these men's responses. She was also impressed by the openness of this fellow Vito who was leading them. Although, she thought, The Bear was a much more fitting name for him. He wasn't arguing with her. He answered her questions directly. This wasn't like the movies or some mafia novel, this was bloody real.

"I've got to say, I'm pretty impressed how you got law enforcement chasing away these assassins, even if it's temporary. I also appreciate that you will get me to where I need to be. I've got to go to Bowdoin College this morning. I need their library. I'm looking for some answers, and I'm positive the answers are at the college."

"Don't know what you're searching for. Don't care," Vito said. "But it better be worth a lot, cause those guys are trying real hard to whack you, and they don't seem like the type to give up easily, if you know what I mean."

"Yes, I know exactly what you mean. Exactly!" Angela said and let out a deep breath, her heart heavy and filled with dread.

Maybe she should just go back to New York. This isn't a movie. This is brutally real. People were trying to kill her. Ironically, the only reason they hadn't succeeded so far was because of the three mafia guys sitting in this vehicle with her. Well…and The Ghost of Bowdoin College had a big part in her survival, too.

What have I gotten myself into?

Vito interrupted her thoughts. "Listen, you've been through a lot. So, let's go grab your things and get you checked out of that motel. I strongly suggest that you try to get a few hours sleep. Pardon me for saying this, but you look like fucking hell. One of the important things we all learned the hard way in the Marine Corps is that, in war, rest is a weapon. Straight from the old Chinese War Lord himself—Sun Tzu. We can watch out for you. And we will. But…yea…I can already tell from your face that it's not going to happen, is it?"

"No, it isn't," Angela said, knowing Vito was right and giving her good advice. "I'm too keyed up to sleep. There is too much to do, and I think people's lives, especially Vincent Mark's, may depend on what I can learn up here."

"Alright," Vito said. "Frankie, stay in the Hummer while I go in with Miss Dominica. Johnny, check her car. It may be wired to explode or have a tracking device. We'll take care of your car and then have it returned to New York, but you, Miss Dominica, will ride with us."

Johnny slid out while Vito accompanied Angela to her room.

"Everything's just as I left it," she said to Vito, hurriedly packing up her things including her notes and files.

Vito, meanwhile, scanned the hall. He noticed five small gouges in the walls, but the slugs and casings had been removed.

Interesting, he thought. These guys were so surprised by us, they covered up the evidence out here but left for another crack at her without scooping up her papers.

When he and Angela greeted the desk clerk to check out of the motel, he was downing a cup of coffee and giving

Vito the once over. "Thought you were a single occupant, Miss Dominica?"

"I was and am, sir. This gentleman and his colleagues are assisting me."

"Doesn't matter to me how many people you have in the room as long as you're paying for them," the clerk grunted. "Just don't want to get cheated."

"I assure you," Angela replied in an even but stern tone, "that I am certainly not cheating anyone, least of all you. I am the only one who slept in the room. Please check it, if you like."

"No, not necessary. And no need to get huffy," he said while finishing printing her bill. "Thank you and goodbye."

Angela put her credit card back into her billfold and walked out with Vito.

Johnny was waiting. "Car's clean, Vito. Looks like these guys got a little lazy or didn't have enough time. No bugs. And no bomb."

"Well," Vito said, "I am concerned they may have called for more soldiers. Anyhow, it's late enough now I can call Joey and find out what he wants us to do."

Vito dialed his boss and relayed the events concisely and completely, like he was taught in the Corps. Joey listened to him without interruption and said only three words when Vito finished, "Keep her alive."

Vito grunted. He didn't like the situation, at all, but it was his job, and he knew it was important or he wouldn't have been asked to do it.

He figured it would take an hour for Joey to speak with Anthony and then get back to him. So, he arranged for Angela's car to be picked up and then had them all grab a quick breakfast at Fat Boy's, a longtime Brunswick landmark.

It was now 8AM, and Angela wanted to get to the Hawthorne-Longfellow Library at the heart of the Bowdoin campus.

"Johnny, you go with her. Frankie, stay in the car and stay alert. And Frankie, I mean it. You keep your fucking eyes open. You let down...you die! Worse...we all die. Remember that. If you spot those guys or anyone like them, hit the panic button on the car keys."

Frankie nodded.

"And Frankie, I want you to locate so you are a good twenty-feet from the Hummer, even though it has eight-feet of solid steel reinforcement and the latest wartime protection the military can buy. These assassins will be looking for you in the car but, you my friend, will be looking for anyone who is looking at the car. The noise from the panic button will startle them, and it will signal me."

With that, Vito turned to Angela, "Look, I'd much rather drive you back to New York right now. That would be the best chance of keeping you and us alive, but if you're determined to stay here —"

"I am," she interrupted him.

"Yea...well...you're Calabrese, so that doesn't surprise me," he said, giving the usual Italian head knock reserved for the people of *Italia Sud*. "If you're determined to stay here, we will do our best to keep you alive until we're pulled off. And listen, nothing personal, but that could happen within the hour."

Vito frowned, shook his head then continued, "This has gotten a lot more complicated, I think, than anyone expected, and I don't see how there's anything in it for us except a damn good chance of getting whacked by some out of town foreign humps. Go do what you gotta do. I'm finished talking."

He turned on his heels and walked off.

Angela was scared, down-to-the-bone scared, but she was stubborn and determined to find what she came to Bowdoin to find. There have to be answers about The Ghost here. It's in the middle of this danger, too. God, what have I gotten myself into, she thought.

I'm an Assistant Attorney General of New York. What am I doing with these mob gangsters? I'm up here in Maine, searching for ghost stories while getting shot at. This doesn't seem real.

Yet, it was very real and, despite everything, something indefinable drove her to put all the pieces together.

"Johnny," she addressed her watcher, "I'm going in that library. Are you coming with me or staying outside?"

Johnny didn't have to think about it. He knew how to follow orders, having also served as a Marine. "For better or worse, lady, I'm your shadow, whether either of us want it or not, so okay, let's go."

The Lady and the Hood walked through the pristine glass doors of the venerable, Hawthorne-Longfellow Library of Bowdoin College, both wondering if they'd be walking out the same way.

Chapter 17

Joey C called Vito back and told him that he had not yet spoken to Anthony One Shot but expected to in the next fifteen minutes. "Listen, Vito, I don't know why Anthony sent a crew up there to babysit this broad, but I don't question The Boss. This must be real important to him, and since it involves Marcantonio, it's fucking double important since Vinnie saved Anthony's life back when they were kids. What I'm saying to you is this…make damn sure she doesn't get hit. Shit, that's the last fucking thing I want to tell Anthony Vacarro, so watch out for both her and your own fucking asses. These guys you're describing don't sound like mamalukes or boneheads. They sound like they know exactly what the fuck they're doing. And…they don't sound like soldiers from another family or cartel muscle, either."

"You got that right, Joey," Vito said, more than agreeing with his boss. "They're good, real good, and I don't know what other resources they might have. If we're going to stay on this, we'll need more men. Maybe the guys in Portland. What do you think?"

"Yea, yea, the Bombacci Brothers. They work the whole Portland region, as I recall, and are tight with Anthony."

Who isn't tight with Vacarro in this business, Vito thought, not daring to share that with his boss. Anthony Vacarro was tightly connected throughout the entire Eastern Coast down to Florida, as well as Mississippi and New Orleans.

They both simultaneously ended their call, and Vito took out his Swiss Army knife. He sliced his prepaid phone card and deposited the pieces in two different trash cans.

He suddenly felt very exposed and looked around. *Fuck!* After getting through Iraq and surviving the bloody shootout in Brooklyn last year, he didn't want to catch a bullet up here in the Maine sticks. How fucking ironic would that be, he mused. Not going to happen, he said to himself. We just have to focus and keep focusing. That's what they drilled into us in the Marines. *Keep your fucking head down and focus.*

Vacarro's awfully smart to only recruit guys who've been in the military and served in combat. Survival is what that experience is all about, and so is this life.

Vito scanned the area, doing a 360 sweep. He then repeated the maneuver, turning in the opposite direction. Then he called Frankie.

"Anything?" He asked.

"Nothing."

"Stay sharp. You sleep, you die," he reminded his cousin.

They snapped off.

Vito assessed the Library. Only entrance was on the side he was on. He discovered the opposite side was administration, the President's Office and the like.

Good, he thought. She's in a very good spot.

He sent a text to Johnny telling him to stay close and that he would watch the only entrance to the library with Frankie scanning the streets.

It was cool weather and still early in the morning, and Vito desperately craved some caffeine, but years of discipline, which had literally kept him alive on several occasions, also kept him from rustling up a cup of coffee.

At that moment, his phone vibrated.

"Vito, yea, I'm confirming that you are to take care of your package and don't let anything happen to it. You hear me?"

"Yea," Vito replied in kind, disappointed and worried but not surprised.

"When she's ready, deliver her back to her place in The City. Then you're done. The Portland guys will call you within five minutes. They're pretty rough around the edges, Vito, but Joey says they know the area well and they're stand up guys. *Capisce?*"

"Yea, yea Joey, I hear you, and I'll be glad to see them. How many?"

"At least five, but you get as many as you need. Watch your ass. You ain't in Greenpoint."

"Don't I know it." The phone cut off...sure enough, in less than sixty seconds.

Vito's phone vibrated again, and a hoarse voice said, "Who's on?"

Vito identified himself.

"Where and how many?"

Vito said five and gave the voice his location. "How long?" He asked.

"Thirty minutes."

"How will I ID you?"

"Portland Seadog cap and ask for the name of Italy's soccer club."

"Got it."

Vito was very grateful for more eyes and muscle. Thirty minutes, though? Got to hold on, he thought. He called Frankie and Johnny to tell them reinforcements were on the way. That cheered up both his guys, although they were too cool to ever let on how much.

"Son of a Bitch," Vito said out loud. There's got to be something really big going down for Anthony to commit these kinds of resources. *And I don't want to know what it is.*

Meanwhile, Angela Dominica was making amazing progress in the library.

Chapter 18

Meanwhile... back in New York City

Vincent was just about to speak, when Anthony motioned him to stay silent.

A young Hispanic tough, about 20-years-old was approaching the two of them. He was clearly nervous, fumbling in the pocket of his long overcoat for something.

"Vincent, stay quiet and stay still, no matter what, you understand?"

"Yes, but...."

"Quiet, remember."

The Hispanic pulled out a large gun and pointed it at Anthony. "Give me your money and that watch. You too," he said, directing his last comment to Vincent.

Anthony calmly motioned to Vincent to do exactly what the kid said.

Vincent couldn't believe what was going on. Anthony Vacarro was being mugged in broad daylight in the middle of Manhattan. Here was the boss of the biggest Crew in The City, if not the country, and he was calmly and peacefully handing over his wallet and watch without a word to this punk. Moreover, Anthony's men, his bodyguards, were nowhere in sight. What the hell was going on, Vincent wondered.

Had Anthony gotten careless? This could be an assassination…not a mugging. He simply couldn't believe it. To his further amazement, he spotted two NYPD officers standing across the street, watching the entire episode, smiling and laughing.

"Vincent," Anthony said, "give the man your wallet and watch, and do it now."

"But Anthony —"

"Now, Vincent."

Vincent did as he was ordered. The kid turned on his heels and ran across the street to a spot not more than three feet from the two policemen, one of whom sported Sergeant's stripes. Then the mugger disappeared around the corner.

Before Vincent could say anything further, the two cops crossed the street, the Sergeant beaming from ear-to-ear.

"Hah! The great, tough and powerful Anthony Vacarro held up by a young street punk. What a joke you are."

"Hello, Sergeant Ryan. Did you set up this robbery?" Anthony asked as if it were an expected, everyday operation.

"You bet your sweet ass I did, you Fucking Scumbag. I recruited that punk and arranged everything, and he took you down. Were you pissing in your pants, Shithead? And who is your asshole buddy here?" He asked, pointing to Vincent. "He doesn't look like one of your usual goons. Are you shaking him down? When word of this fiasco gets around, as to how some two-bit kid took Anthony Vacarro's money and watch in broad daylight, ain't nobody going to respect you anymore."

Vincent couldn't believe his ears. This NYPD sergeant had set them up to be robbed in the middle of Manhattan, while he and another cop watched and gloated. Moreover, Anthony was doing absolutely nothing about it.

"Well, Sergeant, looks like there are still a few of you on the police force who are just as corrupt now as when Serpico was on the streets. No rules for you guys, are there?"

"That's right, Fuckhead, I can do anything I want to street scum like you or anyone else for that matter. You get it? There's not a fucking thing you can do about it. I've got a witness to back me up. Right, Dubrowski?"

"Sergeant, let's get out of here. I don't like being in the open."

"Yea, ok. But just remember, Vacarro, who set you up and know, by this time tomorrow, your name and rep will be absolute shit all over town." With that, Sergeant Ryan and his cohort strolled off, with Ryan laughing all the way.

"Anthony, I don't know what to say," Vincent said, and he really didn't. "I'm amazed how calm you are. Those cops are worse than any street thugs. They're a disgrace to law enforcement anywhere on this planet."

Anthony smiled at his old childhood friend. "Hold your fire, Vinnie. Do you really think I'd allow myself, and you, to be taken down by a street punk, like that? Do you think I've gone soft or lost my balls somewhere along the way? Come with me."

They walked two blocks and turned into an alley. Standing there were four men, including the kid who had just robbed them.

"Here's your stuff, Mr Vacarro. I hope I did alright."

"You did just fine, Riccardo."

With a nod of Anthony's head, one of the other three men handed Riccardo an envelope. Clearly the three were Anthony's men.

"Now take off. Your plane ticket to San Juan is in there. Spend time with your mother and your sisters. Don't come back for six months. Call, before you return, and you'll have a job waiting for you."

"Don't worry, Mr. Vacarro, I may never come back."

With that, Riccardo was off, and the group exited the alley and headed in opposite directions where two black town cars were waiting. Anthony motioned Vinnie into the back of one of the cars. The other three filed into the other car. Before they pulled away, Vincent noticed a Tahoe with four men pulling out two cars behind their town car.

"Your people, Anthony?"

"Yea. Here's your wallet and watch."

"The whole thing was a counter sting, wasn't it Anthony?"

"Yea, all the way. By the way, the gun Riccardo waved wasn't loaded. In fact, it wasn't real; I didn't want him exposed on a Sullivan Act violation. Riccardo got busted on a stolen goods rap, and the Sergeant threw him a deal. Set me up, and his charges would go away. Ryan has been after my ass a long time, Vincent. Riccardo immediately came to my people, outlining what Ryan was going to do. Ryan's a bad cop, Vincent. He's been shaking down smalltime hoods and hookers for a very long time. I called a contact in Internal Affairs. They've known about him for a long time, but never could get the stuff on him. This time, though, they've got him. They videoed the whole thing, and I made my own recording for insurance, a copy of which is now being delivered to them. Tomorrow morning, they'll visit Ryan in his home at 5 AM. He'll be allowed to resign but must leave town and never come back. If he's smart, that's what he'll do. If not, well...you can figure out the alternative."

"Why didn't you tell me, Anthony?"

"Reason one, I needed you to be genuine. If you knew what was going on, you wouldn't have been. Second, the line between the good guys and the bad guys isn't as clear as a lot of people think, probably, including you, despite our youth. Three, and most importantly, I wanted you to experience firsthand that things aren't always as they seem. In short, Vinnie, I want you to get your head out of your ass!"

"Why do you think I'm not in Maine?" Vincent replied, not able to hide the hurt from his voice but understanding why his old friend had done things the way he'd chosen to.

"Vincent, I don't think you're naïve. But you aren't seeing things clearly. You're fucking reacting, instead of acting."

"We're talking about my company, Anthony. My job. Who I am. People are getting killed. Good people, decent people. But, yea, I admit I'm having a hard time getting my head wrapped around all the crap that's going on right now."

"That's right. You're being played, Vinnie, and the play is for keeps. People are getting whacked right and left. How many bodies are there now? Why is all this killing going on? What's the end game, Vinnie? What's the end game?"

"I don't know. I can't figure any of it out!"

"Listen to me, Vinnie, somebody wants your company real bad. That's why people are dying. Whoever is behind this is cutting off the head, knowing that without the head, the body can't function. That's when the predator swoops in and takes over."

Vincent fired back, "But they don't have to kill to get the company, Anthony, all they have to do is offer an extra big premium on a tender offer. No one has to die."

Anthony shook his head. "They're whacking the generals, Vinnie, they are taking out the leadership to insure no one stops them or even slows them down. Whatever you guys have in that company is worth a whole lot to someone, and they aren't taking any chances."

"But I don't know what that could be. Look, Anthony, Sterling Works is a nice, old fashion company. We're profitable, but it's not a lot of profit...not by today's standards. We don't have anything so valuable that people have to be killed for it."

"Man, you fucking Calabrese are hard-headed! *Sei una testa di cemento.* Fucking listen, will you? You are not seeing reality. Your bosses are dead, taken out, that leaves the rest of you unable to stop this takeover. Fuck, you are getting run over before you even know it! So, you've got a choice to make. Either stand down, quit the case, resign and get the hell out of Dodge...or...fight these people while they continue to try to take you out. Either you or they aren't going to make it. There will be only one winner here. *Capisce?* Those are your choices. And by the way, please make up your fucking mind, so I can either help you fight or go back to my business and not worry about your sorry ass."

"But, Anthony, this whole business with The Ghost..."

Vacarro looked away and took two deep breaths. "Ghost, huh...Listen, Vinnie Marcantonio, I've heard the tale of this ghost comes from that damn college of yours up in Maine, right?"

Vincent nodded.

"Well, Vinnie, let me tell you something. I don't believe in ghosts. I may make ghosts, but I've never seen one. So, for me, there are NO ghosts." Before Vincent could react, Anthony went on, "The Catholic Church talks about the Holy Spirit, they talk about the Holy Ghost. I've seen men die, right before me, and, yes, something besides their physical body also gets snuffed out. I don't know what happens to it. Maybe it becomes a spirit, I don't know. But whatever the fuck it is, it must go somewhere. Maybe that's your Casper ghost, the do-gooder. I know he saved your ass twice, according to you."

Anthony wasn't through – he was on a roll. "That's a lot of I don't know shit, but this I do know. You don't run your fucking life by what some ghost, or spirit, or whatever the fuck you want to call it, tells you to do. You don't do that, understand? Now answer my question because you're costing me a lot of money and wasting my time. What the fuck are you going to do?"

Vinnie Marcantonio looked his old friend directly in the eyes and, for a minute, the two of them were fourteen-years-old and Anthony was asking him what he was going to do about some neighborhood bully. As he did then, Vincent knew he could never walk away. Anthony was right, he had to shit or get off the pot, as they so eloquently said in their old neighborhood.

"I'm not walking away, Anthony. I hear exactly what you're saying. I'm not built to quit something, even if it means risking my life. I've got to fight back, but honestly, I don't know what to do."

Anthony smiled, which isn't often. "I knew that's what you were going to say, even before you said it, Vinnie. Some things don't change. Your inner core, your guts. Now stop focusing on what you don't know and look at what you do know."

Vincent brightened from his friend's sage advice. "You're right, Anthony, I'm going about this wrong. I know people are getting murdered, and you are absolutely correct, it must be to ensure this hostile takeover. I know the law firm that supposedly defends us is throwing in the towel. I know the greatest detective agency in the world can't seem to find anything out about this Abba

Corporation who's fronting the takeover. I know the SEC and the Justice Department should be all over this thing...and they aren't. I know the NYPD is treating all these deaths as non-homicides, when they know they're murders. I know this Assistant AG Dominica is the only one who has an interest in this whole mess, and she thinks the ghost story can help us figure it all out. And most of all, I know I can't give up on this thing."

Anthony leaned back in his seat. "See, my fine Calabria brother, you know a whole lot of shit. Now let's head to a secure place where we can figure out what exactly we're going to do next."

"What do you mean we? Anthony, this isn't your fight."

"No, Vinnie, it isn't, but you saved my life once, and I can't let you fight this thing by yourself. Who the fuck knows, maybe your ghost will help us get these bastards."

With that, Anthony tapped the glass partition, pressed on the speaker and told his driver where he wanted to go.

Chapter 19

Back in the Hawthorne-Longfellow Library,
Bowdoin College

Angela was furiously digging through reference materials. She skimmed the early history of the college and any mention or reference to The Ghost.

There has to be something here, if there's anything at all to find, she thought. This ghost started here, and it's related to Bowdoin students and graduates. Where else would I find anything about it?

Given the number of coverups and conspiracies, real or imagined, that seemed to go on in the world, she also thought it entirely possible that Bowdoin's Administration, past or present, knew something about The Ghost, but would more than likely not discuss it.

She pulled out countless reference materials and whipped through them as if she were at a Bloomingdale's sale. Finally, she stopped and thought a moment. She should try the obvious, right? What if she checked the card catalogue for The Ghost of Bowdoin? She almost abandoned the notion; it couldn't be that easy, could it?

Then she pictured who wanted to take her life. She was risking her life for this, so she'd better leave no stone unturned. "No stone unturned," she whispered. Quickly, she slid over to the catalogue, racing through the index. Bowdoin... ghosts... apparitions, then WHAM, her fingers froze. There it was in bold black letters: The Ghost of Bowdoin College.

She couldn't believe her eyes. Her whole body trembled, and her stomach turned upside down. The card referred her to special collections and archives located on the third floor of the library. Trying to maintain her composure and appear calm, while at the same time ready to explode, she swept up her notes and composition book and hurried to the elevator.

When she reached the third floor, she found an enthusiastic and helpful student who was only too glad to help her find the materials. There were three volumes. Angela signed the register, and the student reminded her that non-students were prohibited from removing the materials from the library premises.

Angela moved to an empty study table nearby and opened Volume 1. The Preface began:

"What is contained in these pages and notes is the story of the tragic death of the daughter of a Bowdoin professor as well as the suicide of a Bowdoin student, both in 1805, followed by reports and claims of students and others who were witnesses of extraordinary occurrences of an apparition. Some of these experiences occurred on the Bowdoin College campus, but others happened to alumni, some of whom are among our most distinguished and famous,

well-outside the boundaries of Brunswick. The actions of the various Bowdoin Administrations, namely its Presidents, as well as the records of those accounts are included here. In all cases, the apparition endeavored to assist the Bowdoin person. In no instance did anyone claim they were physically or otherwise harmed. For many years, the Presidents of Bowdoin thought it best to keep these accounts and records from public view, apparently in fear that ghost stories concerning the college may be injurious and damaging to the institution's well-being. Given that there is no concrete evidence or verifiable proof to substantiate any of these stories, it is understandable, if not defensible, as to the policy followed for almost 160 years. However, upon assuming the Presidency of Bowdoin College and having thoroughly reviewed every piece of writing on the matter, I have determined that substantially all of our records, heretofore maintained in confidentiality and secrecy, shall henceforth be made available to the public and open for scrutiny for those who so desire. We shall neither promote nor deny these accounts and records. Wherefore, I have so advised the trustees of my intended actions, and they have voiced no objection."

Signed: James Stacy Coles
January 1, 1963

Amazing. It's all here, Angela thought, as she flipped through page after page of accounts. Jonathan Edwards, his love Mary Howell, Franklin Pierce, Joshua Chamberlain and Robert E. Peary. My God, even Vincent's experience was noted here as was her own. *How did they...?* Then she remembered she had shared her experience with her best friend, and she must have told someone. There were numerous accounts here. Literally, hundreds of pages.

While she couldn't take the time to read them all now, she quickly whipped out her phone and took pictures of President Coles' introduction as well as the initial accounts of Jonathan Edwards. He must be The Ghost. Maybe he's been trying to atone for his sins, his poor judgment which led to a young woman, his great love, losing her life far too soon.

Angela rose from her chair with fire in her eyes and steel in her spine. She'd get to the bottom of this ghost business and right now. Bowdoin had known all along about The Ghost, and yet, they'd done nothing. They hadn't advised parents or students or anyone else, for that matter. Angela stormed out the door of the library with no regard to her personal safety.

Vito spotted her immediately, and so did Johnny. Vito moved with lightning speed and signaled Johnny to stay put and watch the streets.

"Ms. Dominica," Vito said unable and unwilling to hide the irritation in his voice, "where are you going?"

"To the other side of this building," she replied evenly, not about to change her mind, no matter what he thought she should be doing.

"Thanks for the heads up, Lady. You know I'm trying to keep you alive."

Angela slowed and turned to him, realizing she was putting him and his crew in harm's way, too, and said,

"Yes, Vito. I do know that, and I'm sorry I'm making this difficult for you. Right now, though, I've got to see the Bowdoin President. Let's just hope he's in his office on the weekend."

As they rounded the second corner, Vito called Johnny. "Stay put," he said. "She's going in the other side." He then did the same with Frankie and told him to move the Hummer closer.

At that moment, the Portland guys finally showed up, and while Angela entered the Admin side of the building, Vito hurried over and identified himself to the new crew. He positioned the five additional men where he needed them and started to feel a little better, thanks to their reinforcement. Now, he had eyes and muscle covering every approach and hopefully enough firepower to stop any assault on the woman or them.

Inside the building, Angela took the elevator to the second floor where she presented her Assistant AG credentials to the receptionist, who looked as if, judging from her casual clothing, she was just there to do some catch-up work over the weekend. Angela explained in a tightened voice that it was a matter of great urgency for her to see the President immediately. The receptionist tilted her head, smiled and asked her to take a seat so she could relay the message.

Angela had barely sat down when the phone rang, and the receptionist said the President would see her shortly. Angela took a deep breath as she was led to the President's office. She stepped across his threshold ready to attack.

"Ms. Dominica, how nice to see you. And how is Attorney General Travaine? I'm a big fan of his and congratulate you on obtaining such an important position in his department."

"You might want to hold your congratulations, Mr. President. I'm here —"

Before she could finish her sentence, Bowdoin's President did so for her, "You are here to ask me all about The Ghost and the records you've been reading in the library, correct?"

"Yes, that's correct. How did you...? Of course, the library girl called your office."

"Correct, but, actually, I was first alerted when you used the library computer to search Bowdoin ghosts. It's flagged to send an alert to my office."

Somewhat taken aback, Angela regained her composure and tried diving in again. "So...tell me about the coverup. Better yet, tell me everything you know about The Ghost."

"Certainly," he replied. "First, everything I know is in those three volumes. You've probably not had a chance to read them all yet, but I recommend you do. I'm certain you have read Dr. Coles' Preface, of course."

Angela nodded.

"Having digested his message, Ms. Dominica, you now know that there is no coverup of anything."

"But you've never disclosed the existence of these records. You've never warned students, their parents or the public in general. In short, you haven't announced to the world the true existence of a ghost which is right here in Brunswick, Maine."

"Hmmm. That's a lot of accusations, Ms. Dominica. Have you so soon forgotten your Bowdoin education and your legal training? We educate you to deal in facts. So, what are the facts here? Number One: since 1963, all the reports which we have amassed over the years of your 'alleged ghost' have been collected and maintained as a public record, properly indexed in our library, so anyone can find them and read them. Personally, I do not believe in ghosts, and you will agree, I'm sure, that there is certainly no concrete proof of its existence in any of the writings, or you will, I should say, when you have actually gone through the entire collection of materials. So, that said, what are we to announce? Second, and most significantly, as Coles noted forty-nine years ago, and it's been true ever since then as well, no one, not a single person has been harmed or hurt in any of these so-called experiences. Indeed, all the reports indicate that this apparition seems to help or try to help its beneficiaries. You, yourself, have had an episode with this thing, haven't you? And, at no time, were you in any conceivable danger, were you?"

"Yes, but what —"

The President interrupted again, "Were you helped or hurt in your experience?"

"I benefited. There is no question about that," Angela replied, knowing every fact he reminded her of was accurate.

"Then what would you have me do? Spread tales about a ghost that I don't think exists? Warn people about what? No harm has come to anyone in over 200 years. If anyone ever asked about a ghost here, I'd tell them the story we've just discussed and refer them to the three volumes in the library. But no one has ever asked me till now and only help and good things have supposedly occurred with this alleged ghost, if you can believe the tales."

Angela shifted gears. "Ok, Mr. President, I concede that perhaps I was hasty in making accusations against the Administration and for that I apologize. You're right, you are not concealing the information you have. It's not hidden away. It's there, if someone wants to dig for it. At the same time, you're not publicizing it either. But much more importantly, I do believe in the existence of The Ghost, and right now, I think it's trying to tell me something very important. Another alumni Vincent Mark and I are caught up in an unusual series of deaths, seemingly unconnected, with senior people at The Sterling Works, coupled with a mysterious, hostile takeover launched simultaneously against the company. It strikes both of us as being far more than random coincidences."

"I see, and how does your ghost fit in, Ms. Dominica?"

"For one, it gave Vincent a sign that suggests money is at the bottom of all these deaths. For another, The Ghost warned me when two assassins tried to kill me at 3 AM this morning."

"My goodness!" The President exclaimed. "Someone tried to kill you…here in Brunswick?"

"Yes, very much so," Angela confirmed.

"Then we need to call the police right now," he said, reaching for his phone.

"Please don't make that call, Sir. If you go outside this building, you will find a number of very capable bodyguards. I can take care of myself and have plenty of protection. In fact, these men are far more capable of protecting me than twenty police departments. In any event, as soon as we finish this discussion, I'm heading back to New York where I'll also be well-guarded. Thank you for your concerns and for your time."

"Ok, but only because you are an Assistant AG am I following your wishes. I certainly hope you are doing the right thing. Now what else could I help you with before you leave?"

"I think you already have given me what I need. As you said, all of the instances involving The Ghost have centered on it aiding and assisting someone."

"Alleged ghost, Angela, but yes, everyone involved received aid and positive assistance, at least as far as our records are concerned."

"So, if The Ghost tries to show me something, I should listen, right?"

"I wouldn't go that far, but, if you believe in this sort of thing, I'd pay attention to whatever it does or indicates you should do. Read the accounts of Franklin Pierce, Joshua Chamberlain and Admiral Peary. All claim they were given warnings. All listened but Pierce who suffered the consequences in a most heartbreaking way."

"Ok then, again, I sincerely thank you for your time," Angela said, standing up as they shook hands.

The President looked her straight in the eyes. "Take good care of yourself, young lady. We want only good things to happen to our Bowdoin grads."

"As do your Bowdoin grads," she answered with a winning smile. "Besides, I believe I've got a guardian ghost looking out for me."

Angela made a mental note to return and read the manuscripts in their entirety. But she had found what she was searching for, and now it was time to go home.

As she exited the building looking for the Hummer, Vito magically appeared by her side.

"Well, Vito, is your offer of a ride back to The City still open?"

"You bet," he said and grinned. "Nothing would make me happier right now."

He queued up Frankie and Johnny and thanked the Portland guys, who said they'd never had it so easy and sent their regards to Mr. Vacarro.

No assassins were in sight. Vito made a quick call to Joey C., and they were off in the armored Hummer.

As they passed all the beautiful Maine pine trees, Angela dozed off with lots of visions in her head. Unfortunately, not a single vision involved sugar plums.

Joey C's last words to Vito were to get the package back to New York without damage, and that's what he intended to do.

"I don't want any fuck ups, you understand? I sure don't want to explain how a dead Assistant AG was riding in your car, so don't get sloppy. Got it?"

"I got it, Joey. Believe me, I got it!"

Chapter 20

Anthony and Vincent had spent several long hours in the back office of a nightclub Anthony owned, talking and laughing but mostly plotting.

It was really good, Vincent thought, to be with his old friend again. And Anthony relished the opportunity to help his buddy out. Especially when the stakes were so high.

After several beers and a few shots, just like the old days, Anthony said, "We've done enough, now you're coming home with me. No arguments. There's no safer place for you than in my house."

Vincent did not protest. He knew his old friend was one hundred percent correct.

Anthony recognized that people like himself, people who were "in the Life" successful, organized crime figures, were constant targets of two very different types of people – prosecutors and assassins. For the latter, Anthony had a veritable fortress for a house. It was built with steel-reinforced framing, ultra-thick walls, state of the art motion sensors, trip points and an incredible surveillance system.

On top of all that, two of Anthony's men were on patrol all through the night, every night. The shifts were rotated to minimize bitching (although, there was none) and to guard against complacency. No one was "on duty" more than four hours, and they all received an extra bonus for the shift they pulled.

Vincent was given a windowless bedroom and Caesar, one of Anthony's three police dogs who parked himself outside his door.

Vincent immediately fell into a deep sleep. No nightmares, no regrets. That's what a powerful plan can do for the human spirit. It gives the calming sense of hope.

He awoke the next morning at precisely 8:40 AM. Caesar was lying outside his door, just as he left him the night before. The dog was more faithful than most humans.

Rosalie, Anthony's wife, greeted Vincent cheerfully with a warm hug and a smile as big as the sun. "It's so good to see you again, Vincent. It's been far too long."

"Yes, Rosalie, it has been too long, and that's clearly my fault. But I promise you, that will change."

Vincent meant it with all his heart as all of us do in these type situations.

"I hope so, Vincenzo. Anthony is in such a wonderful mood this morning. I haven't seen him so cheerful in a long, long time. It has to be because of you. He missed you terribly, but you know Anthony, he'd never say anything and, of course, he waited until you called him. You men, especially you Italian men, you're such children about these things."

"That we may be, Rosalie, but it's the child in us that all you Italian women love."

"Vincenzo...*Basta!* Enough! But when are you going to settle down with a nice Italian woman and make some *bambini*?"

"'*E basta a te*," Vincent said and laughed. "No more talk of marriage, eh? But, speaking of children, where are yours?"

"Waiting for you at the breakfast table," she said and smiled before continuing, "without Anthony. He went out early but will be back at nine. He asked that you wait for him before you leave, ok?"

"Of course, Rosalie." Vincent walked into the huge Vacarro kitchen, big enough to feed a small army, and no doubt it did on occasion.

All four of Anthony's children were waiting there: Anthony, Jr., 13, Terresa Marie, 11, Donatello, 10 and Louis, 6. Terresa Marie was at the stove along with Magdalena, the Vacarro's resident assistant cook and housekeeper.

The front door sounded with Anthony's return, and there was much fussing and hugging all around.

"Uncle Vincenzo," young Anthony said, "are you going to come see us more often now?"

"Absolutely, Anthony. I have to help your mother and father educate you all correctly. Lord knows you're a handful for any parents."

There was laughter all around.

They talked and ate until Vincent thought he would burst. Then Anthony motioned him to his library, so they could speak in private.

The library was nearly one thousand square feet, with impenetrable sound-proofing, and the oak room was lined with thousands of books of all descriptions and topics. Hardly something you'd expect from a Mafioso.

"I see you continue to confound the popular notion of the Organized Crime Capo, Anthony."

"You mean the books?"

"Yes, there must be thousands of volumes in this room," Vincent said, admiring his friend's collection.

Anthony nodded. "There are thousands. I have an extensive collection on military history, tactics strategy and great battles of the past. In the end, you know, once the fighting starts, all the best laid plans of the greatest generals and kings often mean nothing. The victors are those who can adapt to the changing conditions. Remember what Darwin wrote, Vincent? The species who survive are not the biggest or the strongest, but those who can adapt to change. And Darwin was right. This is exactly what we need to talk about. I have been checking around this morning, and as I told you before, nobody knows anything about any Pros being in town for family business, or for any other business for that matter. Nobody knows nothing, and I got to tell you, Vinnie, whenever this happens, which is very seldom, I get damn worried, because it means one of two things: either it's terrorists or it's government guys on a wet job."

"Are you kidding me?!" Vincent exclaimed. "Terrorists?! Spooks?! What could possibly interest either terrorists or spooks in The Sterling Works? We don't have any operations in the Middle East, and we sure don't have any government or military contracts. This doesn't make sense!"

"Nonetheless, Vinnie, nonetheless! So, let's assume I'm right. What do both these groups despise most? Think about it."

Vincent did as Anthony instructed and the proverbial light bulb exploded in his brain. "They both abhor the light of day. Neither group wants anyone to know what they are doing or why."

"Forget the who they are for the time being, just concentrate on the what they're doing part. These guys have acted swiftly and carefully, and they move before anyone can get a heads up on what they are doing. But now…you know what they're up to."

"Yea," Vincent said, "these guys are killing the top leadership of the company so there can be no effective opposition to the surprise takeover. It will be done before anyone knows anything."

"Exactly," Anthony confirmed. "So, what do you need to do?

"I got it, yes, I see it all now."

"Alright," Anthony smiled and got down to business. "Call your ace snoop at Krill and point him in a new direction. Secondly, get off your ass with that law firm, who's selling you out. Shove a steel rod up their ass and then take them out. Your way, not mine, mind you, although my way would be a lot more effective. By the way, I got a message for you. That AG Assistant you've got a thing for —"

Vincent quickly interrupted. "I don't have a thing for Angela."

"Yea, right, and you call her Angela, not Ms. Assistant AG, how interesting. Anyhow, the girl you're not hot for thinks she's gotten to the bottom of The Ghost business. My crew came back in last night and briefed me. Also, I had a couple of guys watch her place last night, but I can't keep that up. Me protecting a prosecutor?" Anthony grunted. "Sergeant Ryan should have worked with that story. Then, he would have gotten somewhere, instead of sucking wind by getting booted today. He'll be out of New York by tomorrow morning, by the way. Anyhow, the woman, what's her name, Angela, wants to see you right away this morning. Here's her cell number along with a prepaid calling card, to eliminate anyone listening in."

Vincent was trying to process all of this while thinking through his next steps. "I don't know how to thank you, Anthony, I really don't."

"You just did, Vinnie, so stop wasting time and start moving. I'm outta here, and so should you be. I have Terry outside, he'll drive you anywhere you got to go today and then bring you back here tonight. You understand, Vinnie, you're not safe at your apartment and probably not safe anywhere."

"Yea, I got that, loud and clear." Vincent felt fear and excitement simultaneously, and it wasn't a comfortable combination at all.

Almost as an afterthought, Anthony suggested they meet around 3 PM at the carousel on Coney Island in Brooklyn. "I've got to see someone out there this afternoon, and you can bring me up to date on how you're coming along with your plans."

"Good idea," Vincent said. "It's been a long time since I've been to Coney Island. I understand they've done a great job renovating it."

He then gave his old friend a hug, noting the deceptively massive strength in his body, yelled a goodbye to Rosalie and the kids and then and headed out the front door.

Terry was leaning against a black Cadillac Escalade with the back door open. Vincent held out his hand and they shook. He declined the rear seat, however, choosing instead to ride up front.

"Where to Mr. Mark?" Terry asked.

"It's Vincent or Vinnie, please. Mr. Mark...Marcantonio, I mean...was my father."

"Name change noted," Terry said.

"Yea, something like that, Terry."

"Too bad, though, 'cause Marcantonio is a really classy name. Five syllables, musical, you know."

"Yea, I do know. Anyhow, please head to 1177 Park Avenue," Vincent said, hoping Terry would drop the subject.

Chapter 21

Sunday Morning, April 29, 2012
New York City

They arrived safely, apparently without any tail. Vincent entered the building and addressed the smartly dressed doorman, asking for Mr. Leonard Shore II.

"Is he expecting you, Sir?"

"No, he is not, but please tell him it's a matter of great urgency which cannot wait."

Eyeing Vincent extremely carefully, the doorman turned to his telephone while Vincent wondered how someone became a II? *If you're named after your father, then you'd be a Junior, right? How do you get to be a second?* He knew the III follows Junior, but second? *Hmmm...*

"Very good, Mr. Shore, I'll send him right up." The doorman motioned Vincent toward the rear elevator. "Press 'P' for Penthouse."

Of course...the penthouse, Vincent said to himself. I'm out on the streets getting shot at, with my Mafia Capo friend helping me stay alive, and this guy is enjoying his view from the 55th floor, having brunch and sipping mimosas. Something's wrong with this picture.

The elevator pinged and the doors opened to a spacious foyer in which stood Leonard Shore II, elegantly attired in a silk lounging robe.

"Vincent, my boy, kindly excuse my informality, but I wasn't expecting you this morning or anyone else for that matter. Please, follow me. Would you like some espresso?"

"Yes, very much, thank you," Vincent said.

His housemaid Juanita appeared, without him calling for her, received instructions and disappeared as quickly as she arrived. Vincent followed the Vice Chairman out to an outrageously large balcony with magnificent views of Manhattan's skyline. Juanita returned shortly with pastries, which Vincent declined, and a double espresso, which he gladly accepted.

"Well, what's going on with this dreadful business? I assume that's the urgent nature of your unexpected visit?"

"You are correct," Vincent replied. He then went on to describe his findings to date, his assumptions, the basis for them and his strong concern for the physical safety of several Sterling Works' employees, most particularly Vice Chairman Shore himself.

Shore listened carefully, particularly when Vincent said his own life was at risk. "You really think someone would try to kill me?"

"I do, Sir. They've already tried to assassinate an Assistant AG who is simply trying to do her job and help us. They came very close to successfully ending my life, and I'm not a top officer or director. Surely, you are a prime target."

"Hmmmm," Shore poured himself another cup of coffee while he took in all this.

"In fact, Sir, given what I've found, I think it's extremely hazardous for us to be sitting outside on this exposed balcony. We are literally sitting ducks here, especially for professional killers, and believe me, these people are professionals."

"Yes, well, I see what you're saying and perhaps it would be prudent for us to move inside," Shore said, calling for Juanita to come and assist them.

At that moment, Vincent felt a chill, though the day was warm and sunny, and he sensed a presence. He raised his eyes to the French doors and thought he spied a blue-white shape taking a form. It seemed to be beckoning him inside.

Concurrently, Juanita came through the doors. As Shore leaned forward in front of Vincent and invited him to go inside, bullets ripped across the patio. As shards from the concrete patio floor ripped across both her legs, producing a river of red blood, Juanita screamed. Leonard Shore II clutched his chest where a circle of dark red was spreading through his silk robe.

Vincent, distracted by the bluish-white vision, had leaned back in his chair to get a better look at it and had subsequently been shielded by Shore. He pushed sideways out of his chair, holding onto Shore to get both of them out of the line of fire. A second wave of silenced rifle fire erupted.

Clearly there was more than one rifle now spraying across the patio, missing Shaw and Vincent, but hitting Juanita, who dropped to the floor with a thud.

Mrs. Shaw, hearing the screams and unusual sounds she could not identify, rushed toward the French doors to the patio, but Vincent yelled for her to stay back.

"It's gun fire!" He roared. "Call 9-1-1! Do it now!" He screamed at the top of his lungs, all the while trying to maneuver Shore, who was deadweight, behind the table for cover.

A final blast of gunshots raked across the patio, but this time, they hit no one.

Just as suddenly as it had started, everything became eerily quiet. Time seemed to stop. Thirty seconds that's all it had to have been, Vincent thought. Thirty seconds and there may be two dead people plus almost me as a third. In just thirty seconds.

Those fucking bastards! I'm going to get them if it's the last thing I do.

Vincent looked up and across the street for some sign as to where the assassins' bullets had originated, but there was nothing to be seen. The day was beautiful, the sky brilliant. All the other people on the streets and in their apartments continued to go about their Sunday business, oblivious to the carnage heaped upon their neighbors in the last thirty seconds.

If only Shore had listened to him. He then heard him mumbling, and Mrs. Shore yelling from inside. "The police will be here in minutes. My God, my God, is Leonard alright? And, Juanita! Oh my God, Juanita, please get up."

But Juanita was dead, her life ended solely because she was in the wrong place at the wrong time. Happens a lot in life, doesn't it? Bad timing, they call it. Philosophers debate predestination and free will for hours on end, but it doesn't mean anything to poor Juanita. Dead is dead.

Vincent pressed several cloth napkins to Leonard Shore's chest, trying to staunch the flow of blood. Sirens could be heard getting closer, wailing their way to 1177 Park Avenue. Vincent couldn't help but wonder if the officious doorman would wave them through or make them wait until announced.

Get a hold of yourself, he thought.

Shore clutched his shirt and managed to whisper, "Vincent...do whatever you have to do with these people. Do whatever you think is right."

He coughed and gagged. Vincent held him tight, realizing that Mrs. Shore had moved beside him and was cradling her husband's head.

"Don't you die on me, Leonard," she kept repeating.

The emergency teams and police finally arrived, raiding the apartment, relieving both Vincent and Mrs. Shore, who never let go of her husband's hand.

One medic was bent over Juanita shaking his head. "This one's gone, I'm afraid. Notify the Coroner."

By now, even more police were swarming in.

Vincent's cell phone went off, and he answered it in robotic fashion, not even looking at the screen to see who was calling.

"Vinnie…"

It was Anthony.

"What the hell is going on?! Terry said the building is swarming with cops and EMS. He had to pull out of there."

"I'm ok, Anthony, but it was close. I'm going to be tied up here for a while and will probably have to go to the police station to make a formal report. Tell Terry not to wait for me."

"They're really after you, Vinnie," Anthony said.

"They were after both me and the guy I was meeting. He is Vice Chairman of the Board of The Sterling Works and is currently the Acting Lead Director…well…I hope he still is," Vincent said, not sure at all that Shore would live through this attack. "I'll be alright, though."

"I hope that fucking ghost is looking out for you, pal, because you're a magnet for lead these days."

"Yea, he actually is," Vincent replied. "In more ways than you can imagine. I'll still try to meet you at 3 PM, otherwise, I'll call."

"Got it."

And the line clicked off.

By now, a detective was standing next to Vincent. Mrs. Shore had gone with the EMS to the hospital with her husband.

"Can I get some information from you?" The Detective asked.

"Sure."

After several hours, including a trip to the 41st Precinct, where Vincent's statement was taken, transcribed, reviewed and signed, the police were finished with him. He talked with Angela Dominica and briefed her on the horrific developments. They agreed to meet for a discrete lunch at The Princeton Club on 43rd Street where Bowdoin alumni had dining privileges.

Vincent was very careful as he made his way there twenty minutes later. He and Angela arrived within minutes of each other, embraced – Vincent taking note of a definite spark between them. They were seated in a private corner where they had a sweeping view of the entire dining room.

Angela asked about Leonard Shore. Vincent told her he'd spoken briefly with his wife a few minutes earlier, who reported that he was still in surgery and that the doctors were being very guarded about his chances of survival. He also told Angela that both the police and media were covering this as a random attack and not an attempted assassination which, of course, it was.

"How can a sniper attack be random? The fools," she snapped. "Absolute jackasses. Don't they realize all these deaths and attacks are connected, that they all are linked to the takeover?"

"They aren't buying any of it, Angela."

Angela reported that she had tried to reach Attorney General Travaine, but he was in Bermuda for the weekend and wouldn't return until Tuesday morning, although hopefully she could speak with him then. She further

~ 143 ~

described in detail her encounter with The Ghost, Anthony's men who guarded her and her discovery of the three volumes in the Bowdoin Library.

Vincent expressed his shock that the entire collection of records of The Bowdoin Ghost were right there in the open. "The President didn't deny any of this?"

"Not at all," Angela replied between mouthfuls of the Princeton Summer Salad. "He was quite forthright."

"So where does that get us?" Vincent asked. "You know I don't believe in ghosts. Second, even if I did, how can The Ghost help us?"

Angela put down her fork and knife and leveled a steely glare at him. "Well, Vincent, The Ghost has saved your life three times by my count, so even if you deny its existence, it's clear that this thing has been looking out for you, and me, all along. From your description of the encounter back at your office, it also sounds like it was trying to give you a message, as in follow the money."

"Are you saying that this thing is a do-gooder, out to help people in distress?"

Angela edged her chair back and in a quiet, but equally firm tone, responded, "Vincent, I've read the accounts and history at Bowdoin. I believe that this thing is the spirit of Jonathan Edwards, a Bowdoin student in the first years of the college a long time ago. I believe that Jonathan took his own life in a fit of despair and desperation after feeling responsible for the death of his love and intended wife, fellow student Mary Howell. His actions, then and now, are all centered around people connected to the college. I think that he's somehow trying to atone for his actions by helping Bowdoin students and graduates. We have no way of knowing how many Bowdoin people have been aided by his spirit, but there are plenty of accounts in the journals I found."

Vincent listened to the woman seated across from him, wondering how he'd gotten so involved in such a mess. Just a month ago, his life was simple and straightforward. Now people had died, his company was threatened, and somebody out there was trying very hard to kill him and her.

He got mad...Italian mad.

"Angela," he said in a harsh voice that wasn't directed at her but rather was enraged for both of them, "I'm going to fight back. For both of us. For all of us."

He told her what he had in mind. She nodded in agreement and reached across the table to squeeze his hand.

Vincent left first, by design. Angela exited fifteen minutes later by way of an obscure door not regularly used in the rear of the building.

Vincent waited at the front entrance of The Club, pulled out his cell and called for a radio-dispatched town car service which Sterling Works used on occasion.

He impatiently waited with a group of four other men who were arguing about the quality of the New York Rangers. Vincent kept close to them, trying to blend in as if he were one of them. He played the part so well, they offered him a ride, but he politely declined.

By the next minute, he was in his town car. In case he was again being followed, he had the driver drop him off at Grand Central Terminal. He ripped through the cavernous main room full of thousands of people and headed for the Lexington Avenue Subway. Boarding the No. 5 North Train, he got off at 89th Street and walked the long block West to Park Avenue, heading for 2500 Park Avenue, a magnificent, pre-war, gray building with the usual, highly-efficient doorman on duty.

In a commanding voice, he requested the doorman ring Tom Gillis and announce that Vincent Mark was in the lobby.

The doorman looked down his crooked nose and sniffed, "Is he expecting you, Sir?"

"No, he is not, but he'll see me."

Within two minutes, Vincent exited directly from the elevator onto the 50th floor where he was warmly greeted by Tom Gillis.

"This is unexpected, Vincent, but then isn't everything these days. Would you like some coffee?"

"No thank you," Vincent replied, having no time to waste. "I'll get right to the point, Tom. I have tough news for you, so I'm going to give it to you straight."

"What's that, my boy?"

"Tom, first of all, I'm not your boy, and second, you and your firm are out!"

"Excuse me, Vincent? Whatever are you talking about?"

"Out, Tom, as in fired. As of this moment, you no longer represent The Sterling Works. You understand now?"

"What are you talking about, fired? That's insane. We've been counsel to The Sterling Works for over fifty years. This is crazy. Have you gone stark raving mad? I understand that you are under a great deal of pressure and stress, but we are and continue to be the law firm for your company."

"No, you are not. You are fired as counsel. Effective immediately. You see, if The Sterling Works has any chance of being around for another fifty days, let alone fifty years, you guys are gone! You are no longer the lead counsel for us in this takeover. Actually, you're no longer counsel on anything for us."

With that and before Tom Gillis could say another word, Vincent pulled a letter out of his vest pocket, which in all the appropriate legalese, said just that.

In a New York second, Tom's demeanor changed from polite, elite and aloof to street bully. "You little guinea shit, you don't have the authority to do this! You've got some balls! I'll see that you're fired from Sterling and on the street on your dago ass before you can say jack shit!"

"Is that so?" Vincent spoke loudly as he pulled another envelope from his jacket pocket. "This letter is signed by Leonard Shore II, Acting Chairman of the Board of The Sterling Works, with the full endorsement of all the remaining members of the Board. It specifically and unconditionally confirms my authority to fire you and your firm. Looks like it's not my ass hanging out on the street, is it?"

Finally, Vincent pulled a third envelope from his jacket which contained a Notice to the Federal Court for the appearance of the new lead counsel for The Sterling Works in the takeover litigation and a directive for Tom and his firm to immediately turn over all papers and the like concerning the lawsuit to said counsel.

"There's a group of our people at your offices right now, Tom. And by the way, that last letter is endorsed by an Assistant Attorney General for New York, in case, you think you can drag your feet." With that, Vincent whipped out his phone and dialed their new counsel's office giving them the order to immediately seize all Sterling Works legal papers from Black & Lace.

"If you don't comply and provide us with our materials, you'll be subject to subpoenas and legal papers suing you and your firm, which were previously prepared and are in hand at your offices. That would involve a whole shitload of negative publicity and sanctions, which I seriously doubt your firm's Management Committee would welcome."

"You fucking bastard," Tom sputtered.

"That's it, Tom. I'm almost done here. I need you to give the orders to your staff now…yourself. Right now. Do it!"

With an icy glare and a venomous poison seeping through his voice, Tom did as he was ordered, speaking to the associate who was manning the Sterling Works efforts at his firm.

"You've got two hours to turn it all over, although given how little you've actually worked on the case, I would think you'd only need about twenty minutes," Vincent said.

"Why are you doing this, Vincent?" Tom asked, sounding only the slightest bit defeated, although much more nervous than when he was playing street bully moments before.

"Why? I am glad to tell you *old* Tom. Because you've gotten way too cozy with the people on the other side. You're not fighting for us, and you don't give a shit what happens to us. You think we're done; that we're tired, overwhelmed and scared. You hope to be kept on as Outside Counsel by the new owners, whoever they are. Well that's not going to happen," Vincent said, more determined every word he said, "and we're not going to roll over and get buttfucked by these bastards. There's something nasty going on here. People have died. My friends, my colleagues, people I cared about. They're gone. And you aren't doing anything about it. Well that stops now!"

Before Tom could say another word, Vincent turned on his heels and walked out his door. Before he exited, however, he turned back and looked Tom straight in the eye.

"One more thing, Tom...Fuck You!"

Vincent pulled the door shut and exited Tom's home, making straight for the elevator.

Well, that turned the flame up a few degrees, he thought. And it felt good all the way to the lobby, where he took several deep breaths and got control of his emotions.

He pulled out his phone and dialed the Krill team he'd sent to Black & Lace. "Are they giving you the stuff?"

"Yea and pretty quick. There's not a lot of work they produced or research that has been completed, as you guessed. We should be out of here in thirty minutes."

"Good, then full speed ahead!"

Vincent then called Vice Chair Shore's wife so she could fill him in when he was out of surgery and able to listen.

Mrs. Shore chuckled. "I wish Leonard had been there just to see that smug bastard's face. He never liked him and wasn't thrilled with that damn firm. He'd voiced his opinion many times in Board Meetings, but the Chairman and General Counsel both had deep ties with those guys, so you know how that goes."

"I certainly do," Vincent said, "I certainly do."

"Well, the important thing is to keep focused on the game plan now, Vincent. That's what Leonard would want you to do, and if I may speak bluntly, watch your ass. There are a lot of dead bodies piled up out there. I'm so glad you and my husband aren't in the pile."

"Me, too, Mrs. Shore, and thank you for your help," Vincent said.

Next, was a call to Angela which was quite brief.

"I still haven't heard from the AG, but I don't think it will be much longer," she said. "Be very careful, please."

"I will," he answered.

They hung up. Vincent then rang Anthony's newest number.

"I'm done," he said, "and so are Tom Gillis and Black & Lace."

"The boys will be there in ten minutes," Anthony said. "Black Caddy Escalade. And don't take long getting into the car."

"Believe me, I won't."

In less than ten minutes, the behemoth SUV pulled up smoothly to the corner. There were two men in the front seat and one in the back, who opened the door. The guy riding shotgun, and the one in the back seat were both rapidly surveying the streets and buildings for any possible shooters.

In a flash, Vincent raced across the sidewalk and dove headfirst into the car.

"Hey, Vinnie, I haven't seen you move that quickly since high school."

Recognizing the voice, Vincent looked up. It was Tomaso Pappalardo, Tommy P for short. Vincent didn't know Tommy P was working for Anthony.

"What are you doing here, Tommy?" He asked, quickly adding, "I'm sure as hell glad to see you, though."

"Well, Vinnie, I've never forgotten how you pulled that asshole off my little sister our junior year. She was really scared, and you took him out even though he had you by fifty pounds."

"I got a lucky punch in, Tommy," Vincent said, remembering the horrible night very well.

"The way I heard it, you went after him like a pit bull on 'roids. You hit him three times and then kicked him in the balls, and the son-of-a bitch dropped like a fucking rock. Then you took my sister home and stayed with her for hours until she could get herself under control. I was away in juvie detention and then went right into the Marines. When I got out, you were long gone from the neighborhood. I never got the chance to thank you. So here I am, thanking you now."

"Well, it goes both ways, Tommy, because I'm in a real mess now myself. I appreciate your help. I didn't know you were working with Anthony."

As the Cadillac moved along the West Side Highway, veering in and out with the man in shotgun position constantly checking front and back for tails, Tommy P looked out the darkened window and said, "I've been with Anthony about three years now. These are my guys."

They nodded to Vincent.

"They are like brothers to me. Hooking up with Anthony is the best thing I've ever done. Anthony takes good care of his crews, like no one else, you know what I mean?"

Vincent nodded in agreement although he didn't know exactly what Tommy Pappalardo meant and probably didn't want to know. He just remembered him as one of the toughest and most violent guys back in the neighborhood, which Tommy involuntarily left when he was sent to "reform school", although they don't call it that today.

"Last I heard, you went into the Marines, Tommy."

"That's right. The best part was Parris Island. I loved that shit, and I loved the weapons. Did real good with them. But the other bullshit wasn't for me. You know, dumb ass officers who didn't know shit about real field conditions. After I served one tour, I got out and banged around. Anthony saved my ass," he said and paused but didn't provide any additional details. "I'm with him now. Until I go into the ground, Vinnie. Which by the way, we're supposed to keep you out of."

"Good. I prefer topside, Tommy."

Chapter 22

Later that evening, after Tommy P and his crew had delivered Vincent safely back to Anthony's home, and after Rosalie had cleared the dinner plates, Anthony gave his wife a big kiss on the cheek and said, "Vincent and I are going to talk in the den, okay?"

"Sure, Anthony," she smiled, knowing this meant no interruptions from her, the children or anyone else, short of all-out assault on the house.

Anthony led the way down an unusually long flight of stairs, through a fortress-like door which was at least a foot thick into a large, comfortably-furnished room. It had the look and feel of a man cave, without evidence that a woman had ever stepped across the threshold, but it also had no windows.

It registered with Vincent that this was most probably a secure location, both from the standpoint of electronic eavesdropping as well as assault. No doubt, Anthony had a concealed exit passage somewhere. His old friend may not have gone to college, but he had a lot of smarts you don't get from an Ivy League school.

"You want a little Grand Marnier, Vinnie?"

"Yea," Anthony replied, "straight up."

"*Salute*." They toasted each other.

Anthony then looked at Vincent with that piercing gaze of his, reaching almost to his very soul. "So, tell me, my old friend, why did you change your name?"

Vincent wasn't expecting this question and somewhat taken aback. Given that his emotions were running pretty wild the last several days, he wasn't prepared to discuss yet another topic that unnerved him. "Of all the questions to ask me, Anthony, why would you pose this one again?"

Without getting a reply, Vincent continued, "As I told you at Patsy's, Anthony, it seemed like the right thing to do, at least at the time. I felt I needed to move along in the legal world, and it just made things a little easier career-wise."

"You changed your name because you're trying to escape your heritage, where you came from. You want to distance yourself from people like me and the old neighborhood. You're ashamed of who you are, and you've been trying to run away from it. Now, you're in a shitload of trouble. And who is trying to keep your skinny ass alive?"

Vincent physically stepped back, stung by Anthony's words. "Listen, Anthony, you don't need to be my bodyguard." He moved toward the door to exit the room. "Forget I ever called you."

Anthony blocked his way and wasn't budging.

"Sit down, Vincent, and have another drink. You're going to listen to what I have to say. I am going to try my damnedest to protect you and that thick, Calabrese concrete head of yours. I am your friend. I will always be your friend. You saved my life. I will never forget that. I'd be lying if I said I wasn't hurt when you stopped all contact with me, but I understand what you went through after your parents died. And I even get what you were trying to do to class yourself up. But you are who you are. You have nothing to be ashamed of. Nothing. You are one of the good guys, Vinnie, and there are damn few of them."

Vincent momentarily stopped breathing, simultaneously relieved and shaken. He sat back down with his oldest and best friend and accepted another glass of cognac.

"Let me ask you this, Vinnie, when you told that blue nose Wall Street lawyer to go fuck himself, when was the last time you felt so good?"

That made Vincent laugh.

"Now, tell me this…was that guy Vincent Mark talking, the hotshot corporate attorney, or Vinnie Marcantonio from Brooklyn?"

Vincent thought for a long moment then smiled and said, "Anthony, you always did know how to cut through the crap and get through to me. The answer is that I felt like I was back in the old days, and it was a Marcantonio, not Mark talking. There's no question about that. The truth is, I'm not sure about a lot of things I've been doing before all this happened. I'm even beginning to think that stupid ghost might be the real thing."

"Well," Anthony said, "that's a start, a good start. Now the more pressing question is…are you committed to this mess or do you want to disappear? Frankly, if you get out of town, I think those guys will forget about you. They're hired to take you out solely because you're fucking up their plans, which are, you know, to take over the company you work for. And the thing is, Vinnie, that would be the smart play. Just bow out. Be a whole lot healthier for you, I guarantee it."

"I can't walk away, Anthony. I just can't. I guess it's the Calabrese in me."

"Yea, I figured as much," Anthony smiled, "and maybe it's a little of that pretty Assistant AG, huh? At least she's Italian."

"Maybe it is a little of her, too, Anthony, but I just can't give in to a bunch of thugs and killers."

"You never could, Vinnie. That's what I always liked most about you. You are pure guts," Anthony paused and then continued, "you know what Caesar said when he crossed the Rubicon and headed into Rome with his army to face Pompey and his Senate buddies? *"Alea iacta est."*...Latin for the die is cast."

"Anthony, where do you come up with this stuff?" Vincent said, always amazed by his friend's ability to quote all kinds of people on a variety of subjects.

"I read a lot, my friend, so let's leave it at that. Now, no more alcohol. I figure tonight is when these guys will try to hit this place, since tomorrow is a big day for you with that Federal Judge. I normally have one or two of my boys on watch every night and none of them ever knows, until the last minute, which ones. It reduces the chances of someone being bought off, which has never happened, mind you, but then Caesar didn't think he would be stabbed twenty-three times either, the last blow by his own adopted son, Brutus."

"Listen, Anthony, I don't want to put Rosalie and your family at risk. I should go back to The City."

"You're kidding, right? My family is at risk every day of our lives. Have you forgotten what I do for a living?" Anthony said and laughed. "Tonight, I'm gonna have an army around this place. Ain't anyone going to get within one hundred yards of this house. I put in extra, state of the art surveillance cameras and silent motion detectors as well. Been meaning to do that for a while anyway. Come on and follow me over to the Control Room. It rivals all the alphabet agencies."

Anthony moved over to the opposite wall, hit a remote he was carrying, and the entire wall slid open, the pictures and mirrors all disappearing. He beckoned for Vincent to follow him.

He pressed another button, and lights flashed on instantly, revealing a rather large room closely resembling a security control bunker. There were computers, monitors and all kinds of sophisticated technology and equipment.

"Sit down, Vincent."

Vincent did as he was asked, realizing his mouth was still hanging half open, in awe of the entire techno theatre surrounding them.

"Right out of the movies, isn't it?" Anthony asked, beaming with pride.

"The Matrix or something like that," Vincent whispered. "This must represent a small fortune."

"Yea, it does and worth every penny. Since you showed up," he said and grinned, "I upgraded and enhanced an already state of the art system," he said, sweeping his arms across the many panels and devices. "Basically, this place is as secure as Fort Knox and far more secure than the White House. Basically, I have cameras, sensors and motion detectors all around the place. No one can get within one hundred yards of this building without me knowing it. And whether it's an 'unfriendly' as opposed to a stray dog attempting to approach, I'm sent a warning signal no matter where I am. Plus, Rosalie is thoroughly comfortable with this stuff, although I'll admit, it took her a long time to learn, and she kicked and screamed the entire way. She hates computers."

"Yea, but this is amazing," Vincent noted, never imagining Anthony would need this level of protection, which didn't make for the easiest of feelings.

"See, Vinnie, I can do a lot of things here, but tonight, I need to be ready for a full frontal, professional assault. They know you're here, and they're coming for you. We're being watched right now, which is why, my friend, it's time for you to leave, and I don't mean by the front door."

"Wait a minute, Anthony, I can't leave you, Rosalie and your children, I — "

"Shut up, Vinnie. You will leave and leave right now. This is the safest place on this planet for my family. Rosalie will be fine, and my children are learning about survival in a hostile world. You are at risk, so you're going to a "Safe House" as the Feds like to call them, where you can get ready for court tomorrow. Tommy P and his boys will take you, watch you all through the night and deposit you in that courtroom tomorrow at 10 AM sharp. They've already collected all your papers from your house, and here's a throwaway cell to make any calls to that Italian AG you're sniffing around. Don't give her the number. It's blocked. You make the call to her. Don't describe where you are, either. Got it?"

"Yea, but I got a lot of questions," Vincent said, knowing Anthony's plan was the best chance he had at making it out of this whole mess alive but beyond disturbed knowing the danger his friend and his family were in because of him.

"*Basta cosi,* Enough," Anthony said. "You know all you need to know. When this is over here, I'll call you, no matter what time. No conversation just our word "*Bellagio!*" He said and smiled.

Bellagio is a beautiful village on the shores of spectacular Lake Como, in the north of Italy. When they were growing up, Vincent and Anthony would fanaticize about traveling to that magical place. For them, it was kind of like heaven, where everything was good and sweet. It had become their code word for 'everything's alright'.

"So, get your ass moving, Vinnie, and be ready for tomorrow. After firing your lawyers earlier, and given what's going down tonight, they are going to come at you with an army of lawyers and tricks tomorrow, so be prepared. Think about all the ways they will try to beat your butt in."

"Yea, I will Anthony and...," Vincent started to get a little choked up and couldn't finish his sentence.

"Get outta here. Now!"

With that directive, Anthony led him to the south wall of the control room where a gigantic map of NYC was hung on the wall, not a digital map, but the old fashion paper kind mounted on a firm backing. Anthony hit another button on his remote, and the map moved up revealing a small compartment. He pushed Vincent in.

"When the door closes, count to ten, then the floor will start dropping. When it stops, the door will open. Get out and follow the tunnel. There are a number of fire stops and alternative dead ends, but you just follow the right side of the tunnel," he said. "When you get to the end, there'll be a ladder, about twenty feet high. Think you can still climb it, or have you gotten too fat and lazy?"

Vincent laughed nervously, not in denial that, indeed, he was out of shape.

"When you emerge from Dante's Inferno, you'll be in a warehouse. Walk to the front and go through the green door to a small office. Turn left and exit into a garage area. Tommy P and his crew will be there in a white panel truck, with the back open. Get in, and Tommy will drive you out."

"Anthony, I don't know how to thank you."

"You can buy me a bottle of Montepulciano when this is all over. But pay attention, Vinnie, because this is far from over. Watch your ass and do what Tommy says. He's crazy as hell, but he knows how to stay alive, and he loves you like a brother ever since you saved his sister that time."

Vincent looked at his old friend and smiled. "*Ciao, fratello.*"

"*Ciao, Vincenzo. Buona Fortuna.*"

Vincent stepped into the lift, and the panel closed him in. Then he counted to ten and felt the drop.

"Here goes," he said to himself.

At the same time, Anthony turned on his heels and headed for the master console, where he would direct the ensuing battle. After first speaking to his wife, via a secure communication device, to make sure she and his three youngest children were in the bomb shelter, he opened the door, so his oldest son could join him; after all, he had to make sure Anthony Jr. would be ready to take over as head of household, if his father were killed.

Chapter 23

Later Sunday Evening, April 29, 2012
New York City

Meanwhile, Angela Dominica had ended her conversation with Vincent on a very worried note.

"Be careful," she said, and at the same time, realized she also needed to be careful.

Violent men had already come after her. They were ready to kill her. Just because she hadn't seen them in 48-hours or so, it didn't mean they weren't around.

At that present moment, she was in the middle of Grand Central Terminal at 42nd street. Pretty busy place to kill someone. On the other hand, it could happen.

After Vincent's call, she had tried her office again, but still no response from her boss, the AG, who presumably was still in Bermuda. Yet, she thought, surely, he would have a few moments to return a phone call from his employee, especially knowing who it was, on an assignment he had personally given to her.

This just doesn't make sense.

She started to get pissed. Not mad, not angry, but pissed off, Italian style. Well, screw him, she thought, if he isn't going to look out for me, then I'll look out for myself. All in, as they say. Hell, she was getting more support from The Bowdoin Ghost than from the Attorney General of New York or from the NYPD, combined.

Vincent and she had plotted a hasty plan over their lunch at The Club, which seemed like days ago, rather than a few hours. Angela headed downstairs for the Lexington Avenue line, swiped her subway pass and waited a respectable distance from the edge of the platform for the uptown express. It roared in, and she stepped inside, luckily getting a seat, so she could scan the people around her to see if anyone was following. She kept this up until 59th Street, where at the last minute, she hopped out and scurried up the subway stairs to Bloomingdales.

Moving as fast as she could in four-inch heels and a fairly tight, straight skirt, she headed for the second floor and zeroed in on a non-busy saleswoman. She explained what she needed, and the woman was very efficient with her help, although a little puzzled. But this was New York City, after all, so strange was the norm.

Twenty minutes later, Angela exited Bloomingdales a completely different woman. Now, she was in a gray running suit, with a NYC white baseball cap and her hair piled under it, sneakers on and a backpack with both her purse and her stylish suit and blouse, rolled up inside. She had placed the illegal spray can of mace and the four-inch gravity knife she always carried with her in the outer pocket of the backpack, so she could easily access both.

With this accomplished, she felt better and hailed a taxi, checked the rear view and had the driver speed to 14th Street where she hopped out and literally ran to the subway entrance, descending the stairs and heading to the Houston Street stop where she exited.

Carefully checking her surroundings, she called her old Bowdoin roommate who had an apartment at Hudson and Houston. Angela explained that she needed a place to crash for a few hours. Since her friend was out of the country on an extended business trip for the next month, there was no problem. Both had each other's backs in case of any need, and long explanations were never required. When Angela was safely inside the apartment, she collapsed in one of the deep-cushioned chairs.

Angela breathed deep, letting her lungs empty out fully each exhale. Her pulse slowed. She focused on not thinking, which was the best way she'd found to clear her mind, so she could think without clutter and allow her subconscious to horn in and guide her.

A single image came to her mind: The Ghost.

Maybe Vincent Mark didn't think it was real, but she did. Instinctively, she felt he really did accept the notion of an honest to God spirit moving around out there, but he couldn't acknowledge it to anyone, even her.

Ok, she thought, if The Ghost is real, it's been warning us of danger. But what else? Money. Yes. But money in what way? How does it connect with The Sterling Works?

Then...there it was... her big eureka moment. Of course, her brain fired back! It's something the company has, and apparently, its officers don't know they have. Someone wants that company because it is the door to a lot of money. What could it be – oil, gold, a patent, some old documents with valuable real estate that no one knew they owned? It could be anything, she thought.

And it wasn't something she, or anyone else, was likely to figure out in the short term. But one thing was very clear, however. Someone powerful was willing to kill a lot of people, important people, so the prize must be of enormous value.

Maybe it's not even money. What else could it be, though? Something of historic importance, or more likely, something which leads to a lot of power and, in turn, leads to a lot of money and privilege.

Ugh! All this is so frustrating, she thought.

She breathed more slowly, and her mind cleared. I'm sure that whatever it is that The Sterling Works owns, it will come down to money, power or most likely both!

The only way to thwart these people is to stay alive to prevent their takeover, and at the same time, figure out exactly what it is that they, whoever the hell they are, are so intent on obtaining.

She then turned her focus toward the next big questions...

Why haven't the NYPD and the Feds acted like all this killing is a big deal? They are basically doing nothing. And why hasn't my boss called me?

She slapped her forehead so hard, it gave her a brief headache. He isn't too busy. He's been warned off. The police aren't all over this thing because there's someone who is so powerful they can make the NYPD stand down. It's the Feds, or more precisely, the NSA, or any of the alphabet agencies, probably crying national security or terrorists.

Well, she thought, what's clear for sure is that the court date tomorrow is crucial. And she had an idea how she could help. If the AG wouldn't even talk to her then he certainly couldn't tell her what she could or couldn't do in regards to the case, right?

With that, she smiled for the first time in many hours. Then she called her brother.

What Angela did not know is that she had been tracked ever since she'd left lunch with Vincent. Two Swiss mercenaries, one male the other female had been within a short distance of her. The female tracker had even followed her into the changing rooms at Bloomingdales, thus, she was fully-knowledgeable of Angela's quick makeover.

As Angela began the conversation with her brother, the female Swiss assassin was outside the door to her apartment.

By now, Angela had explained to Matteo that she was in danger and desperately needed help. Fortunately, Matteo was only about fifteen minutes away having a beer with two of his friends. He heard the distress in her voice.

"Stay calm, Sis, and I will come get you."

At that moment, the assassin rang the apartment doorbell, wanting to make sure she had the right apartment before acting further.

Matteo heard the buzzer in the background over the phone and quickly said to his sister, "Angela, do not go near the door."

Rebecca, the tenant and Angela's old roommate, had a pre-war fire escape outside the bedroom window.

"Go out the window, Angela. Break it if you can't open it. I'll meet you on 8th at 14th street. Go now!"

Angela replaced the receiver and felt bile rising from her stomach. There was no reason for anyone to be ringing Rebecca's door at this hour. She could smell fear oozing out her pores. Her brain realized danger. It was screaming at her to run.

As the buzzer sounded again, she swiftly moved to the bedroom. Fortunately, the window wasn't painted shut, nor was a security bar in place. Out she went, even as she thought she heard clinking sounds from the apartment entry, which was probably the assassin picking the lock.

Angela was already climbing down the escape, which wasn't visible from the front door. Two things helped her: first, the entry door had two deadbolts, top and bottom, which slowed the assassin's work. Second, Angela had purchased two sweatshirts and caps at Bloomingdales, and had changed into a bright red one with a white cap, as soon as she had gotten into Rebecca's apartment. If someone bad was coming for her, she'd thought, they may know I'm no longer in gray, but they wouldn't know what color was next.

In fact, Angela had a third piece of good fortune in that the assassin stopped trying to break in, since the door wouldn't budge, and she didn't want to attract any neighbors' interests in the noise she was making in the hallway. One of them had already poked her elderly head out into the hallway to see what was happening.

In eight minutes, and on a dead run, Angela was on 8th Avenue, and there was her older brother with his two buddies, speeding to the curb.

"Hey, Sis, what the hell is going on?" He asked, as she piled into the back seat of his black Honda Pilot.

"Just drive, Matteo, just get us away from here as quickly as you can."

Matteo didn't question his sister anymore, he just mashed the accelerator.

Chapter 24

Anthony had been staring at his computer screen for several hours now and had finished off two black coffees, no sugar. He wasn't tired, though. His adrenaline rush was still at peak levels. That was the old Marine in him. *Never let up! Never give up!*

He checked again with each of his crew, making sure they were alert to the coming attack. There was no doubt in his mind that the moment was close at hand. His survival instincts were on extreme alert.

"Remember," he told his crew again, "no hesitation. It's eat or be eaten."

At that precise moment, Sensor 3 went off, and Antonio knew the enemy had engaged. The Mother Fuckers think they're going to kill me in my own house. They're in for a big fucking surprise, he harrumphed.

Three more sensors went off on his screen, picking up intruders, and then a fifth and a sixth sounded. Six in all, he relayed to his men, giving them precise locations of each.

Anthony had a total of ten of his best soldiers in the field. He didn't believe in overkill, but he did believe in the tactic of superior numbers. Usually, but not always, the guy with the most guns wins, but he didn't know exactly how many combatants would try to blow up his house and everyone in it. So, he overcompensated.

"Donnie, Chickie, you got one enemy almost on you, he's moving right past you now."

All of Anthony's men were fitted with night-vision goggles, and all their firearms were suppressed. Unfortunately, so were the intruders. This was going to be a very quiet, and more than likely, a very short battle.

Donnie took down his mark with two shots. Chickie eased over and put two more in his head, in case he was wearing body armor, which he wasn't. Chickie relayed this fact immediately over the wire.

Three more pings, and an additional combatant coming in from the East went down, clearly dead.

That's two, Anthony noted.

The remaining assassins were moving quickly toward the rear door. One peeled off his weapon with a shoulder movement, retreated and stopped advancing. The other three had suppressed AK-47's in their hands and concussion grenades hanging from their belts.

This neighborhood's definitely getting dangerous, Anthony thought, with a wry smile.

Unknown to Anthony, a stray bullet hit the upstairs kitchen window. Since he'd had all the windows made bullet-resistant some years ago, there wasn't any breakage. Nonetheless, no one wants their family getting shot at.

At the same time, a black clad figure with a rocket launcher was sighting the Vacarro back door when the cold metal of a Glock 9mm was pressed against his temple.

"Lower the rocket, asshole, or your brains are going to be all over the fucking place."

With that, the assassin dropped his weapon and was hit hard enough to lose consciousness before he was dragged off.

Meanwhile, two of Anthony's men had located the nondescript white van that delivered the assassins. The driver was looking down at his weapon on the center console when he was shot twice in the head through the window. Anthony's men bypassed the locked door with a jimmy tool, got in and pushed the dead driver over to the other seat. They then drove off carefully, not wanting to arouse attention from anyone, especially in a neighborhood where NYPD patrol cars and the occasional FBI Agent kept tabs on the Vacarro residence.

Curiously, the Federal Surveillance Team which normally tracked Anthony, had been pulled off the assignment a week ago, right after Vincent Mark had met with him in Manhattan. That did not escape Anthony's notice.

It was 2:23 AM. Nine minutes had elapsed since the attack had commenced. Anthony knew they were now looking at the end game of this adventure, but he also knew that's when things can often change in a nanosecond; that is, when defeat becomes victory or apparent victory turns to disaster.

There are three professional killers left, he thought. That's still a lot of fire power. A grunt came over the headphones as one of his men was spotted and shot in the arm. Leonardo Savage ran to his friend, firing every round in his clip.

Meanwhile, the other two assassins were now fully-alert to the situation. They stopped their advance and started backtracking while spraying the terrain with automatic fire.

All this was happening and yet no gun shots were heard by anyone in the neighborhood. A casual observer would have muttered "hell's bells, all's well", since from his or her perspective everything was.

Anthony's heart was pumping fast now. He didn't want any of these bastards to escape, and he didn't want any of his men killed trying to stop them.

"Savage, what's the story with Prutzi? Is he hurt bad?"

Nothing.

"Savage, do you hear me?"

"Yea, Boss. Prutzi is hit. The bullet grazed and seared his arm, the Lucky Prick, now he'll be bragging about his new scar," Savage said and laughed.

"Listen to me, all you guys, take out those three remaining. Dead, alive, or in between, but none of them walks away from here. You hear me? Nobody walks off!" Anthony's voice was tight with tension and determination. It was as if he were back in Iraq under attack from the enemy. He had the ability to stay totally focused in a firefight while the world was blowing up all around him. That skill had saved him and his fellow Marines on many occasions.

The headphones cracked again. "I got one, Anthony, and he ain't going to be talking – no way."

"Two left," Anthony barked. "Get them."

As the seconds ticked by, Anthony wondered if his men had remembered their military training and would cover the escape route to the white van, which now of course, was no longer there. He needn't have worried, though. Two of his crew, along with two reserve men who had been waiting in a black SUV, had the location completely blanketed with a classic, interlocking field of fire.

As the remaining two assassins emerged from the darkness to the street where they believed their getaway vehicle was, they were cut down in a blazing hail of death.

"All accounted for, Boss," reported his field leader Michaele. "Only one survivor, and he's on his way to The Center."

The Center was a desolated warehouse across the Hudson in the Meadowlands, New Jersey. For obvious reasons, the location was not identified, but all of Anthony's men knew it well.

"How's Prutzi?" Anthony asked.

"He's ok. Already headed to the hospital."

It wasn't a city-licensed hospital his soldier was talking about, but rather the crew's state of the art outpatient facility, staffed as needed with doctors and nurses, on Anthony's payroll. Their services were extremely well-compensated, and all were blood-relatives of family members. It was highly unlikely any of them would talk about their lucrative healthcare services.

Anthony knew that Prutzi would be in good hands. There would be special bonuses for all of his men who took part in tonight's situation and an extra bump for Prutzi since he had been wounded.

Plus, the word would get around that somebody had tried to hit Anthony unsuccessfully, and his crew had taken out everyone involved. No man left standing would be the "report". This sort of unofficial press notice helped to discourage future attempts on the Vacarro crew.

Anthony scanned the boards one last time. Everything was back to normal. The entire firefight and attack had lasted less than fifteen minutes. A lot of living and dying can happen in fifteen minutes, he thought, as he shut out the lights in his Control Room, put his arm around his oldest son, and headed upstairs.

First, he gave the clear signal to his wife and young children, who emerged from their fortressed room without any questions. There were never any questions. The entire family had absolute and unconditional faith in Anthony.

Next, he told Donnie to bring Chickee with him and meet him in the front of the house in the Suburban. The rest of the crew would stay all night on watch, in the unlikely event, another attack was attempted.

"Not bloody likely," he said to himself, "they lost too many soldiers tonight. They aren't likely to come back here, but I'm always prepared for the unexpected, and I never assume. You assume something can't happen, and then it does. And you're fucked."

The Suburban pulled up, and Donnie got out holding the door for Anthony.

"You're going to monitor things from the cave for the rest of the night," he told him, taking him by the arm and bringing him inside his house. "There's plenty of hot coffee and sandwiches. Don't fall asleep. You can rest tomorrow, and then take your family down to Disney World for a long weekend…on me. Just keep my family safe. *Capice*?"

"You got it, Boss. The action is over for tonight, most likely, but if anyone comes back, we'll be ready. I'll bring in six more of our people who have been on close standby, just to make sure we can handle anything that comes up."

Anthony then turned and headed for the Suburban. He saw old Mr. Amantea on the sidewalk with his cane and his little dog, Nicky, a male Maltese.

"Hey, Mr. Amantea, what are you doing out here? It's after three o'clock in the morning, no place or time for you to be roaming the streets."

"Anthony, I couldn't sleep, so I told Nicky we'd get a little exercise. You know, he doesn't like anyone except me, you and my late Rosa, God bless her soul."

Anthony smiled and said, "Yea, well, Nicky's a good judge of character, I think, Mr. Amantea. He doesn't trust anyone except those that can be trusted. You okay, though, feeling alright?"

"Just this damn arthritis, Anthony, but I'm still above ground, and so are you. Looks like somebody was trying to change that tonight."

Again, Antonio smiled. Amantea didn't miss much despite his 83 years.

"I knew something had gone down, but here you are as always. Won't they ever learn, Anthony? *Ciao, Antonio, e una lunga vita.*"

"*Ciao*, Mr. Amantea, and same to you and Nicky."

When Anthony closed the door of the SUV, Chickee, who had moved over to the driver's seat said, "Anthony, it's pretty late for Mr. Amantea to be roaming around, even in this neighborhood. I know he was one of the Big Bosses in the old days, but I'd worry about him now."

Anthony laughed. "See that cane he's using, Chickee? It's got a steel-point shaft with a hair trigger in the handle, and he carries a close-range Beretta in his left pocket. Besides that, the old guy wears a bullet proof vest under that shirt, I kid you not. Believe me, he's ok. We're in more danger than he is. Now drive. We got to have a serious talk with the asshole who tried to kill us tonight."

Once underway, Anthony, pulled out a SIM card, popped it into his phone, activated it and sent a one-word message to Vincent: *Bellagio!*

If Vincent was awake, he'd know everything was okay, and if he was asleep, he'd wake up to good news. That was their old code word for 'things are fine'. If they weren't fine, the message would have been: *Caesar.*

It shouldn't have taken Anthony and Chickee long to get to their New Jersey destination, but they didn't speed nor run any lights. Frequently, they checked the traffic around them but saw nothing remarkable. They were extra-vigilant at the New Jersey toll booth, too. After *The Godfather,* all the wise guys were careful with toll booths.

When they reached the warehouse and drove inside, it was 4:15 AM. Anthony's men had already noted their presence on the cameras located around and inside the facility.

Anthony spent a small fortune on the latest technology for all of his properties and employed his personal, Italian "IT Department". If anyone or thing approached the warehouse, they would be instantly detected, and an escape route activated if necessary. Otherwise, any uninvited guests would be liquidated. The property was owned by a Cayman company whose stock was, in turn, owned by a Lichtenstein corporation, the shares deposited in a Swiss bank. Nowhere did Anthony's name appear on any deed or register.

The same was true of most of his assets. He had been told by a tax lawyer long ago, if you want to keep things simple, then you'll pay Uncle Sam the max; if you want to legally minimize your tax obligations then you're going to have to have a complex structure. That platinum advice pretty much applied to all of Anthony's business and dealings. The thicker and more tangled the web, the harder to get through the jungle.

Juries didn't like complicated financial and corporate structures. They liked things simple, so there was no reasonable doubt to mess with. Lesson 101 in the "Brotherhood Handbook".

As Anthony climbed down the ladder concealed in the northeast corner of the gigantic facility, two of his men were waiting for him with their prisoner, along with "Doc", one of his hospital staff, who had an impressive mobile medical bag with him.

"Ok, let's get started," Anthony motioned to Doc and then turned to his prisoner. "Listen, you're a hired soldier sent on a mission. You and your group failed. All your team is dead. You are the only survivor. Your associates attacked me in my house where my family lives. That's a big fucking mistake. A very big fucking mistake! You've got one chance, and only one, to see the sun rise. Doc here is going to give you some drugs. They're going to help you tell me everything you know. Don't fight them. Let them wash over you. Spill everything you know. You understand me?"

The prisoner nodded.

Anthony continued, "We aren't going to torture you, we are not going to beat the shit out of you or carve you up. Are you listening to me? But whether you live or die depends on giving me every piece of fucking information you got. Don't try to be a fucking hero, either. You do this for the money, I know, and maybe you get a little thrill, but there's no thrill in dying and no amount of money can bring you back from the dead. Got it?"

Again, the prisoner nodded, and then he spoke, "I will tell you everything I know. You don't need to use the drugs. I will tell you everything."

"Good, good," Anthony said. "That's the smart play." He looked at Doc and motioned for him to begin.

Forty-five minutes later, Doc and Anthony had emptied the mercenary of every bit of knowledge he possessed.

The entire group was fifteen strong. They were all Swiss nationals, professional soldiers who had mustered out of service and had been recruited by a para-military group for hire anywhere in the world. Their boss was in Zurich, at The Dolder Grand Hotel, waiting for an update. Their target was Vincent Mark, and they had followed Vincent to Anthony's home.

They knew that Anthony was involved with the New York mob, but that made little difference to them. If his family or anyone else had to die in order for them to kill Vincent, so be it. Classic collateral damage. The pressure was on them from their boss in Zurich. The orders were to take out Vincent tonight, so that he would no longer pose a threat tomorrow in the court room or with the takeover of The Sterling Works.

Also, a separate team of two was assigned to kill Assistant AG Dominica. The mercenary did not know why these people had to die, only that these were their orders. He also confirmed that all the other Sterling Works' officers who died recently were assassinated as well by their team.

He did not know who had hired his company except for one fortunate piece of information he had been privy to. His boss had uttered a curse at the conclusion of a phone conference with the client. He'd said: "...the fucking Chinese. I really hate working for the fucking Chinese."

That was it. But that was a lot considering the cut-out mechanism and the need-to-know policy these assassin groups religiously practiced.

Anthony sent Vincent another one-word text, "*buon giorno*", which was the signal for Vincent to call him on the burner phone. Anthony also called Tommy P, the soldier who had never left Vincent's side that night, even when he was sleeping.

Anthony told Tommy P to get Vincent up and that he would be there in thirty minutes. Things were moving very quickly now. The Assistant AG may already be dead, he thought. He did a quick check-in with his crew back home to make sure no one else had tried to attack the place, which no one had.

"Well, one benefit out of this," Anthony mused. "As word circulates around town, I doubt any competitors are going to try something anytime soon against our family. And that's actually quite good for business."

With the streets quiet, and The City just beginning to shake off the night, Anthony arrived in record time at the designated safe apartment he'd put Vincent in. He filled Vincent in on the details of the last several hours.

Vincent wanted to interrupt several times but didn't, knowing he should listen as carefully as he could until Anthony finished.

"Clearly, I've got to warn Angela," he blurted out. "God, I hope nothing has happened to her."

Anthony interjected, "How were you two communicating? Remember, these Swiss bastards are sophisticated. They track cell phones. They know where she lives. Before you go rushing off to God knows where, how did you leave things with her?"

Vincent got a hold on his emotions. "You're right, Anthony. I've got to think more clearly. I'm not very good at all of this anymore, am I? We agreed she would come to the hearing this morning at 11, as an observer from the State of New York."

"Okay then, give the woman some credit. She knows they tracked her before and tried to kill her up in Maine. I'll have a couple guys go look for her. In the meantime, give me her cell number. I'll have it called remotely and tell her you're proceeding as planned and that she should watch out for her pretty little butt. My people will deliver you to your hearing, but they are not going in the building. You gotta manage that part on your own. Can you do that, Vinnie?"

"Yea…yea, I can handle that," Vincent said, hoping that hearing himself say the words would help him make it happen.

Chapter 25

Monday Morning, April 30, 2012
Foley Square, New York City

One hour later, Vincent Mark was on his way to Federal Court, Foley Square, fifth floor, before Judge Matthew T. Brody, a veteran on the District Court who had handled numerous securities cases, including hostile takeover litigations.

As Vincent sprang from Tommy P's Suburban and dashed up the steps, he had two of his men with him. He made the entrance without incident, and his minders parted company at the massive entrance.

Vincent looked around. It seemed business as usual in the hectic lobby. He walked calmly to the line for attorneys, emptied his pockets before the metal detector and passed through without sounding an alarm. He collected his personal items and his briefcase on the other side and headed for the stairs.

"These guys, whoever they are, surely can't be reckless enough to try to kill me here in Federal Court. They can't be that crazy," he muttered, trying to convince himself. "And yet, that is exactly the unexpected thing to do, isn't it? Don't let your guard down." *God, I wish Anthony was here.*

Vincent was rounding the third staircase, with no one else in sight, when the apparition appeared once more. He stopped dead in his tracks.

"Oh shit! It's happening again, and I'm not hallucinating," he said out loud. *I'm not crazy! Damn, Angela was right about this thing!"*

The Ghost moved toward him, clearly signaling that he should turn around. Vincent's instincts kicked in, and he spun around, scurrying down the stairs back to the first floor.

His heart was racing, his breathing rapid. He was sweating. He could taste fear oozing from his body. His brain suddenly kicked in...The Ghost is warning me. There is danger upstairs!

On the busy ground floor, he pulled out his cell and rang his Krill contact.

"Justin," he said. "I need your help."

He quickly explained his concerns about an ambush and ended the call.

Two minutes later, one of Justin's assistants, who Vincent recognized, along with another Krill employee and two Federal Marshals, popped out of Elevator #3, and Vincent quickly joined them.

The bigger Marshal said, "Sir, what happened?"

Vincent colored his answer a bit, not about to reveal his encounter with The Ghost. "I was climbing the stairs and saw three suspicious men waiting for me on the fourth landing. They were definitely up to something."

"Can you describe them and..."

Before the Marshal could finish his sentence, Elevator #4 opened with a shooter bringing his automatic weapon to firing position. Simultaneously, two others, similarly clad in fatigues, were racing down the stairs, also with raised automatic weapons.

All hell broke loose. The assassins' weapons were not noise-suppressed, probably intentionally, to create even more chaos. The noise was deafening. Screams, cries, people diving to the floor in every direction.

The Marshall talking to Vincent went down, as did one of the Krill men, the latter's face exploding all over Vincent.

After what seemed an eternity, the courthouse guards began to return fire. They were no match for the assassins, however, who also had the benefit of full-body armor.

"How the hell did they get into a secure Federal Court Building?" Vincent wondered.

Vincent's fight-flight survival response kicked in, and he lunged for an open elevator door as the automatic weapons continued to spew death and destruction indiscriminately. He shook as his fingers finally hit the fifth-floor button, and bullets pinged off the closing steel doors.

"Thank God for old time construction. These steel doors are thick."

His mind went back to the scene he had left behind. "How many innocent people had been harmed, maybe killed, because of me? These monsters that will stop at nothing!"

The elevator bell sounded at the fifth floor, and the doors opened to a surreal calm, as no one here was yet aware of the melee below.

Before stepping forward, Vincent peered out. His legal team, including Justin Krill, two more Krill employees and Vincent's new counsel saw him coming and raced toward him. The noise five floors below hadn't reached this level yet, but Vincent's phone call to Justin had, and this group was in total confusion as to what was happening.

Warning alarms kicked in and screams could be heard coming from outside the building.

Vincent, slightly out of breath and very pale, managed to say, "It's a blood bath down in the lobby. There are at least three men shooting."

Before he could say more, Judge Brody burst from his chambers and ordered everyone out of the corridors. "The police and FBI are both on their way up here. We've been advised that a terrorist group is trying to free Muhammad Kalil, who is being arraigned on the fourth floor. Everyone inside. The bailiffs are locking all doors."

Vincent knew that this incident had nothing to do with terrorism or the person being arraigned. But what a clever cover for these guys. They were going to kill me coming up the stairs on the fourth floor and lay it all on terrorism.

Meanwhile, the building was now seeing every kind of law enforcement possible: FBI, NYPD, Swat teams, Anti-Terrorists Specialists and more.

Of course, the three assassins were long gone. They left the same way they entered – by the roof, where a Sikorsky helicopter had been waiting for them. How they were able to accomplish this on a supposedly secure Federal building was a complete mystery…never solved.

Vincent decided it was not in his interest to contradict the authorities' version of what was taking place. First, he couldn't prove anything, nor could he identify anyone attacking him. He had nothing to substantiate a claim that these men or those who had attacked Anthony's home last night were all part of an elaborate assassin squad somehow connected to the attempted takeover of The Sterling Works.

Like so many things in life, what he knew to be true could not be verified, and what he did not know could not be ascertained. Perfect chaos. Vincent's report would simply subject him to endless hours of questioning and law enforcement files being opened on him.

About an hour later, Judge Brody looked around his anxious courtroom. "Bailiff Roskoski, the door is still secured, correct?"

"Yes, Your Honor."

Two Federal Marshalls were stationed on either side of the massive wooden doors with weapons drawn at the ready.

"Well, Ladies and Gentlemen, it appears all the parties are here for The Sterling Works hearing on substitution of counsel and whether to continue the temporary restraining order against the Defendants preventing the takeover offer. I note that our stenographer is at her station, and I see no reason why we can't proceed. Clerk, would you please call the case?"

Vincent, of course, had no time to coordinate with his team, but threw caution to the wind and prepared himself for the moment they'd all been waiting for. Hell, The Ghost had just saved his life again, so he was feeling a little more confident to proceed. He didn't have much more to lose. Maybe the Judge understood that time was critical here.

Justin leaned over and in a hushed voice said, "Full speed ahead, Vincent, give 'em hell!"

For the next thirty minutes, Vincent was simply brilliant. After the preliminaries, including a halfhearted effort by counsel for the defense to postpone things because of the chaos in the lobby, the Judge permitted the substitution of counsel, pleased to do so because no time extension was required by Vincent's new legal team.

Following the conclusion of the first matter, the Judge was handed a note by his clerk, which he seemed very uncomfortable with. He finished reading the note then addressed the room that they'd be taking a short recess.

Judge Brody, looking particularly stern and somewhat ashen in color, returned to the bench shortly thereafter, and said, in an extra-booming voice, as if to further legitimize his authority to do what he was about to do, "We are on the record, Ladies and Gentlemen. It appears that we are experiencing an extraordinary event here at Foley Square, and I don't believe it is prudent to continue proceedings today. Accordingly, under the circumstances, I'm going to postpone this hearing for seventy-two hours. During this time, the restraining order against the Defendants will continue in full force and effect, preventing their tender offer from moving forward, and finally," he said, addressing the counsel for the defense, "I do not see the witness you were ordered to produce from the Abba Corporation. Is he or she present?"

"No, Your Honor, we — "

Interrupting, the Judge said, "Your reasons do not matter. I've read your brief, consulted caselaw, and the law is clear on this point. You will either produce a Senior Officer of Abba Corporation for examination by the Plaintiff and this Court, or I will make the temporary restraining order a permanent injunction. The parties are hereby ordered to return here on Friday, at 10:00 AM. Are we clear, Counselors?"

Each side muttered perfunctory acquiescence, and the Judge left the Bench in a rather hurried manner. Just before he reached the door to his Chambers, he said in a loud voice, "Before leaving, I urge each of you to depart from here with care and safety. Above all, you are to comply with all appropriate directives from law enforcement officers."

Just like that, Judge Brody disappeared into his chambers, leaving Vincent and his team somewhat speechless.

"Listen, Vincent," his new counsel said, "as far as today is concerned, despite whatever is going on downstairs, the hearing could not have gone better for us. You got new counsel approved, the restraining order stays in effect and the Judge gave a clear signal that he'll book no bullshit over all the secrecy regarding the people behind this takeover."

"Yea," Vincent said, in agreement, but without much enthusiasm.

Part of him was still reeling from how close he came to meeting death, yet again. But for The Ghost, it would be him splattered all over the fourth floor.

"You're right," he said, temporarily snapping out of his dark mood. "We did well today, but what will they do now? They can't go forward without producing a senior principal for examination, right?"

"That's right, Vincent, but if they do, we'll nail their collective asses to the wall."

Vincent smiled at the idea, but not without numerous reservations and concerns. These guys weren't going to be stopped by this, they'd produce someone who would lie like Judas. Perjury isn't going to worry people who kill without conscience.

He turned to Justin Krill. "How is your investigation coming?"

They looked to make sure opposing counsel wasn't within earshot. "Honestly, we're bogged down right now.

We've traced the holding companies to Lichtenstein but can't get any further. The registry people in Lichtenstein are not cooperating at all, and they aren't even trying to hide their stonewalling. It feels like a Swiss move…with great power and a lot of money behind it…maybe China."

"Why do you say that?" Vincent asked.

"Nothing concrete, just years of experience, and my gut, but I doubt the real parties of interest in this thing are revealed at the next layer of discovery. This thing has the earmark of a deep concealment, like the ones governments operate. Like the Chinese. The Swiss are just the first line of defense, but a formidable one. They do this for the money, but it would have to be an enormous amount of money for them to be this committed. They are the best in the world at hiding things. Think WWII."

"Why," Vincent wondered out loud, "why have these people, whoever the hell they are, gone to such extreme measures, including multiple murders, to take over one insignificant, rather boring company?"

To Vincent's surprise, Justin quickly answered him. "Vincent, The Sterling Works must have something of enormous and incredible value. So valuable, in fact, and so powerful that very desperate people are willing to kill to obtain it. You just don't know what you have. Find out, and it will go a long way to solving this bizarre mystery."

Vincent nodded. He's right, absolutely right, but Vincent didn't have even a remote clue as to what that highly valuable asset could be.

"Ok, everybody, good job under trying circumstances. Let's go back to work. I need to brief our Acting Director as to what happened here, and then I'll check in with each of you about 7:00 PM tonight, okay?" Vincent said.

The door to the courtroom swung open somewhat violently as a regiment of police and Federal agents swarmed in with weapons drawn. The agent-in-charge held up his badge and ordered everyone to take their seats, while a team of cops checked ID's, searched bags and recorded names and addresses. A second team of swat members scoured the courtroom, checking every nook and cranny, including entering the Judge's chambers without knocking. That brought a rather vociferous response from His Honor, despite his earlier directive to everyone else to cooperate with all law enforcement.

After an hour that felt like four or more, Vincent and his group were free to leave and were escorted to the front of the Federal building. Vincent immediately spotted Tommy P and headed for him.

"What the fuck, Vinnie?! You really got a rasher of shit following you. When I called Anthony and gave him the news about the attack, he nearly took my head off on the phone. I told him I put you right inside the courthouse myself."

"Calm down, Tommy, it wasn't your fault. These guys are working overtime to take me out, and they know what they are doing. If it wasn't for Anthony and you guys, they would have succeeded long ago."

"Hold on, Vinnie, I gotta call Anthony, and let him know you're okay, and that you're with me right now."

Two of his soldiers were hustling Vincent into another armored SUV. Vincent used the time to call Leonard Shore, who was slowly, but surely, recuperating in the hospital. He briefed him on everything that had occurred. They agreed to talk again at 8:30 AM the next morning.

Tommy P. passed Vincent his cell, and Anthony asked him how he was holding up.

"Okay, Anthony, okay. I think I'm more pissed off than scared, but I know what has to be done. It's just as we discussed yesterday and last night, my choices are clear.

Either disappear or beat them. I'm not disappearing, so it's war, but I do want to make sure Angela is okay. I don't even know where she is right now. I didn't see her in the court room."

Anthony grunted, "She's with her brother in an East Side apartment. I've got three guys watching the place. Tommy is taking you there now. Listen, Vincent, I got a funny call. I can't talk about it now, but I think it relates to your mess. By the way, the guys who have been doing all the killing, they're Swiss."

"Swiss," Vinnie repeated, learning that Justin Krill's hunch was right.

"Yea, Pros, of course, military training, the elite type. They're not going away, either. We need to get to the bottom of all this fast, and I mean fast."

For the first time in several days, perhaps ever, Vincent heard apprehension and a restless urgency in his old friend's voice. Not fear...but a very deep concern.

He was relieved to hear Anthony talk about "we" getting to the bottom of it, instead of just him. Yet, he was trying to repay a debt that he never owed.

He didn't care what else Anthony Vacarro did or was doing now in his life, he was a real friend. And he was *his* friend. The kind that's there no matter what, not just when times are good or bad, but no matter what, they're there. Very few of that kind exist on this earth.

"I'll call you from Angela's, Anthony."

All the while, Tommy P. was chattering away. "Hey listen, Vinnie, I know you're up to your neck in piss and alligators right now, but when I told my sister about seeing you and all, she nearly had a stroke. She made me promise to ask you to meet her for a cup of coffee or a drink, anything. She's never forgotten you, as I told you, and I think she's always carried something in her heart for you.

What do you say? Can you meet her, after you get over whatever you're involved with?"

Vincent smiled. No matter how bad his life was right now, he wanted to see Sofia. And he could sure use a nice diversion. Who knows, he thought, maybe he'd always carried a thing for her in his heart, too.

"Tell your sister, I'm extremely flattered, Tommy, and that if she's available, I'd love to meet her for a drink. How about 9:00 PM tonight at Four Seasons?"

Tommy P was beaming. "Thanks, Vinnie, it would mean a lot to her, and it'll keep her off my ass. I'll even take you there myself and make sure nothing happens to you. I promise you that."

"Good deal, Tommy."

And with that, Vincent took a few deep breaths and closed his eyes for a moment. Perhaps he was beginning to understand who he really was. And he was a lot happier for it, even if a bunch of bad guys were trying to bury him.

He called Angela on the burner phone. He could hear the tension in her voice. She was very glad to hear from him, and he quickly updated her on the chaos at Foley Square as well as gave her the scoop on the hearing. She was well-aware of the chaos at the courthouse from all the media reports, which continued to cast the incident as a terrorist attack.

Vincent didn't mention what happened at Anthony's house the previous evening. He would wait until they were face-to-face...or maybe it would be best to omit it entirely.

Within fifteen minutes, Tommy P. proudly delivered him to Apartment 3G in the Armstrong Building on York Avenue.

"Vincent, thank God you are here and you're okay," Angela gushed as she wrapped her arms around him and squeezed as hard as she could, which was quite a lot.

Chapter 26

Anthony Vacarro had received a lot of strange phone calls in his life, but the one from Internal Affairs Detective Gates was certainly among the top ten.

All the detective would tell him on the phone was that he wanted to meet him, and that it had nothing to do with their recent encounter.

Anthony was puzzled and concerned. Nonetheless, he agreed to meet the detective and arranged for extra protection from his crew. Not that he thought he was in physical danger, but he was always a careful guy. Care had kept him alive.

Detective Gates had not wanted to meet in any of Anthony's usual locations, and he didn't want any public place where they might be captured by a surveillance camera.

So, Anthony and four of his men arrived at Grand Central Terminal at 5:30 PM, thirty minutes early. The crew took up their posts and communicated with each other through various, ultra-sophisticated devices.

Detective Gates arrived right on time.

The two men nodded to each other.

"Vacarro, I'm going to give this to you quickly because I don't think either one of us want to hang out and be seen together."

"Agreed," Anthony said, "what's up?"

"Quite a lot but let me give this to you straight up. With everything going on, I'm telling you this, not because I like you, because I don't. I'm still going to try to lock you up for the rest of your life. Hey, you're not wired, are you?"

"No, that's more your kind of thing, isn't it?" Anthony replied with the smallest of smiles. "But should I be?"

"Don't get cute, asshole. I'm doing this for three reasons. First, you were straight with me over the Sergeant Ryan situation. Second, your buddy Mark is in a shitload of trouble. I'm talking big, big trouble, and from what I know, he's a decent guy, not mobbed up."

The second reason got Anthony's full attention.

"What kind of trouble?" He asked.

Detective Gates didn't answer him.

"The third and most important reason I'm telling you this is we cops don't like what's going on with all these murders. The Sterling Works and your friend Mark seem to be in the middle of it all."

Anthony winced. "You think Vincent Mark is causing all these deaths? Well, let me — "

Before he could finish, Detective Gates cut him off, "No, I don't think that, but shut up and listen to me. I...uh...we...don't think Mark is the cause; in fact, he's the prime target to be the next victim. What the NYPD is pissed off about is that we are being told to stay out of it. Fuck! Stay out of all these murders and shit going on in OUR city?! So is the FBI. They are completely barred from any involvement. They don't even have a team assigned.

It's an order directly from the Secretary of Homeland Security."

Anthony showed no emotion, but his brain was going at full speed.

"Haven't you thought it fucking strange that we've got all these people getting killed and no cops are out there investigating? Not one! No FBI. Barely any press coverage. And the blood bath at Foley Square had nothing to do with terrorists. Those guys were after Mark, but I'm sure you and he know that."

Vacarro chose not to respond again, wanting Gates to keep spilling information.

"Here's what has the Department, even guys like me who are way down the power ladder, worked up...The Police Commissioner and the Mayor are livid that their hands are being tied. Respond, give us your reports and stay the hell out of our way is how Homeland Security is ordering us. Personally, I don't think the Commissioner is going to put up with this much longer. The Mayor comes from the same party as the President, but he's not far behind the Commissioner in being fed up. Whatever is going on must be huge. I've never, in all my years, experienced anything like this. Seems to me the pressure to get rid of Mark is at the red line. Frankly, I hate to see him get whacked because the police are being ordered to let it happen. Oh, and Vacarro, tell your buddy that his Judge isn't coming back, either. He's towing the line, which means I wouldn't be surprised to see him gone before Friday."

"Are you saying a Federal Judge is going to get hit?!"

"No, you moron, they don't have to kill him, just yank him. You get it now? Our fucking Federal Government is pulling all the strings here and allowing our citizens to be taken out, as in killed, and a Federal lawsuit to be manipulated so a takeover of a company can occur. There, I've got it off my chest. I hope you got Marks under lock and key, Vacarro, 'cause they are out to get him. And there are a lot of them. But my conscience is clear, even if I'm pissed off to high heaven."

"Thanks, Gates, I appreciate the information."

"I didn't do it for you, you know," he said.

"I know that, but thanks just the same."

After parting the station, Anthony called Tommy P. to make sure Vincent was under wraps. He learned then of the 9:00 date. "Put him on, Tommy."

"Hey, Anthony, what's up?"

"Quite a lot, Vinnie, but let me get this straight, with everything going on, you're messing around with the Dominica woman and you're meeting Tommy's sister for a drink tonight, in a public restaurant? Are you even remotely aware that people are deadly serious about taking you out, and if anyone else happens to be in the way, they're gone as well?"

"Yes, Anthony, I am aware."

Vacarro laughed and said, "Vinnie, you're sounding more and more like your old self every hour. And I like it. Alright, I know why you want to see Sofia as she's got the hots for you. She never got over you from the moment you saved her. You've been her hero. Go ahead, and I'll make sure you're covered, but just for drinks and one hour, no more, then the guys will bring you back to my house. You'll sleep there tonight."

"Listen, Anthony, I've been talking with Angela, and we both think we've got to go back to Bowdoin. She's convinced that a lot of answers to what's going on are there."

"Son-of-a bitch, Vinnie! Alright, but she stays with us, and in Maine, she sticks with the program to the letter, *capisce?*"

"Of course, Anthony."

Vincent explained that he was to rendezvous with the legal team at 7 PM tonight and with Director Shore at 8:30 AM tomorrow.

Anthony ran his fingers through his hair. "You know, Vincent, taking care of you and trying to run my business is turning me gray, but what the hell, I guess you're worth it. Don't worry about transportation to Maine, I'll take care of it, and you and Dominica will be ok because I'm going with you. No argument. Let her know that, right now. It's non-fucking negotiable."

He waited while the message was relayed.

"She says okay, in fact, she smiled, and her brother agrees as well."

"Alright, I'm coming over now. I'll be there in fifteen minutes. I have some very important information for you. *Basta* and *Ciao.*"

Anthony and his four bodyguards were on York Avenue in less than ten minutes. By then, Angela's brother had left, after making her promise to keep him informed as to what she was doing. She promised, lying with the sincerity only a good Sicilian can muster.

Angela and Anthony shook hands. "Well, now I can say I've personally met the famous Anthony Vacarro and am actually going to sleep in his house."

"And I can say, I've finally met the beautiful and smart Assistant Attorney General Angela Dominica, who is going to sleep in my house."

Angela smiled. "Yes, correct on both points."

The three sat down at the kitchen table and Anthony began sharing what he had learned, without revealing how or from whom. First, he gave Vincent a name. It was the assassin who was captured at his home. Trace him through Krill right away. He's Swiss, and I think you'll find out who he works for. Second, I'm pretty sure your Judge is going to be pulled off your case."

"You're kidding?!" Vincent cried out.

"I wish I was," Anthony replied.

Angela chimed in, "How could you possibly know that?"

"I don't know, for sure," Anthony replied, "but you better get prepared for a new, unfriendly Judge who'll give you no support."

"Shit," Vincent said.

"Plus, there's been a lockout of all local, state and federal law enforcement, by Homeland Security, in all these murders and your litigation."

"Why? What the fuck is this really about?" It was Angela's turn to toss out a few curses now.

"That's the question, isn't it?" Anthony asked. Without answering it, he continued, "and last, it's absolutely clear, Vinnie, that your company has or owns something of immense and enormous value. Something that would cause a foreign power to commit multiple murders and stop at nothing to achieve their end game with tacit help from people at the highest levels of our own government. And, Vinnie, let me tell you that, I don't think any ghost, real or imagined, can stop these people."

Vincent frowned deeply. "That's what's driving me crazy. I don't have a clue as to what these people are after."

"Well, they want your company because your company has what they want," Angela said.

"Now," Anthony said, "if I had a problem like that in my business, I'd start tearing apart the books. Somewhere, in your records, your balance sheets have an asset worth billions. Maybe trillions. Get your books. Or at least get the digital versions."

Vincent had momentarily forgotten how all-around savvy Anthony was, a high school dropout who could quote Caesar – in Latin – and take apart the latest hardware and unravel its software.

Immediately, he got on the phone with Krill. Then he phoned Leonard Shore.

Shore had already scheduled a telephonic meeting with the remaining board members for 9:00 AM, thirty minutes after Vincent would have his phone call with him in the morning. Shore said he would have the finance team pour over the financials in search of the mysterious, prized asset. He also said he would have all the statements, records, ledgers and balance sheets, including assets, downloaded onto a flash drive, so Vincent could work on them before the meeting, with all the data in his pocket.

By then, Vincent had heard back from Krill. The name he'd given them was that of a professional assassin with Swiss nationality who was part of a unit which reportedly worked exclusively for the Chinese government. Supposedly, it was a Black Ops Group that is utilized when the Chinese do not want any of their citizens involved in a sensitive mission that could cause an international incident. Justin said these are very dangerous people. "Vincent, we are talking about *the Chinese* here."

"Is that who is behind this?" Vincent asked.

"Probably so," Justin replied.

Vincent paused, "Are you still with us?"

"Hell yes! All in!" He said.

With that, Vincent, Anthony and Angela felt they had made some real progress.

Anthony stepped into the bedroom to take care of some personal business and checked in with his men watching the apartment.

Vincent told Angela about his meeting with Sofia set for 9:00 PM, not because he had to, but because it felt like it was the right thing to do.

"Time to go to your meeting," Anthony said, coming back into the kitchen.

"Wait, it's only 7:45, Anthony."

"Yea, well, I've moved your reunion up by an hour. We've got a big day tomorrow, and you need your beauty sleep."

Angela smiled. "Yes, the earlier it is, the less it seems like a date, so the less jealous I'll be. You don't want to make a Sicilian woman jealous, do you, Vincent?"

Vincent was surprised by her remark, but glad she expressed feelings for him, even if in jest. He clumsily mumbled a reply, and both Anthony and Angela openly laughed at his boyish awkwardness. Then, what the hell, Vincent laughed as well.

Chapter 27

Monday Evening, April 30, 2012
The Four Seasons, New York City

Once Vincent was securely inside Four Seasons with five body guards, Anthony and two of his men took Angela to her apartment, sneaking her in the back way, so she could collect what she needed for the next several days.

Sofia lit up when she saw Vincent. She hugged and kissed him so hard, repeatedly, he was afraid they were attracting attention. He hurried her to their table, sat down and ordered drinks – a beer for him and a glass of white wine for her.

"God, Vincent, it's been years. You look absolutely fabulous. I'm so happy to see you, even if it's only for an hour. I'm not even going to ask you why you haven't called any of the old gang, but I know why, too many are gangsters today."

"It's great to see you also. And wow have you grown up. You are gorgeous, Sofia. I mean it."

Sofia was beaming.

"There's so much to catch up on, I don't know where to begin," Vincent said.

"Actually…I do, Vincent…I can't thank you enough for what you did back in high school. I…"

"Sofia, please. There is no need to bring up unpleasant subjects. Tell me," he asked, switching gears, "Tommy said that you're not married. Is there someone special in your life?"

She smiled. "No, there isn't, and Tommy told you that, I'm sure, because I asked him to make sure he did. I think I've always been waiting to see if you and I — "

"Hold on, Sofia."

"Don't worry, Vincent. No bum's rush, but you opened the door with your question. Now then…tell me why Tommy says you're in some kind of trouble, and that you were at Foley Square when that awful attack took place."

With that, they talked nonstop for a solid hour. No awkward pauses and no regrets. He was Vinnie Marcantonio again. Life was much simpler. Truth be told, he would be much happier as that guy all the time.

At exactly 9 PM, Tommy appeared.

"Oh, Tommy, go get lost for another hour, we're having so much fun," Sofia pleaded.

"I'd like to, Sis, but The Boss gave strict orders. We got to keep this guy healthy. You want to see him again, right?"

"Yes," she said and looked at Vinnie, "I would like that very much."

"Give me your number, and I'll call you," Vincent said.

"Sure, but I know what that means," Sofia said unable to contain the disappointment from her voice.

"No, No," Vincent replied with a deeply serious face. "I'd like to see you one week from today, same time, same place, but for dinner, not just a drink. So, I need your phone number."

Sofia was ecstatic. She fished paper and a pen from her handbag and passed Vincent her number. "It's a date, Vincent. God, I can't believe this."

"I'm really looking forward to it as well," he said, and he was.

The three walked out of the lounge, and as they said their goodbyes, Sofia leaned in to Vincent and pulled him close to her body, giving him the most exciting kiss he'd ever experienced in his life. His legs started to go weak, and he didn't want to leave her.

"Oh man," Tommy quipped, "you guys look like you need a room, and I'm the asshole that's got to break it up. Come on, Vinnie. Go home, Sis."

"Mind your manners, Big Brother, this is a special moment for me." With that, Sofia kissed Vincent again, and this time, he definitely didn't want to leave.

Finally, with Tommy's assistance, they parted.

"From the looks of things, I think my sister's got it bad for you, Vincent. Try not to break her heart."

Still in shock from their volcanic kiss, Vincent replied, "Believe me, Tommy, she is the last person on God's Earth I would ever want to hurt."

Tommy checked the time again, then they exited Four Seasons and rushed into the waiting SUV.

Shortly thereafter, Tommy P. delivered Vincent to Anthony's compound where Angela Dominica was engaged in an animated conversation with Anthony's wife, over the merits of the Calabrese versus the Sicilian recipes for marinara sauce.

"Hey, Vincent, this one is some kind of woman. Beautiful and smart...and...she knows how to cook," Rosalie said.

"What else can you ask for, right, Anthony?" She asked and laughed, but then just as quickly changed her mood.

"Wait a minute, let's remember where he's just been, having a drink at Four Seasons with an old girlfriend."

"Hold on to yourself," Vincent interjected, "she was not a girlfriend, just a friend, and I did it for Tommy P., so he wouldn't bug me crazy."

"Hmm," Angela said, "your just a friend seems to have gotten lipstick all over you and your shirt, but no matter. We modern, Sicilian women are not jealous, I told you that earlier."

Anthony snapped his head back and said, "You believe that, Vinnie, and you're not half as smart as I know you are."

They chatted about all the events of the past few days and then decided to turn in early. Anthony said he was pretty sure no one was going to attempt anything again here, but he was well-prepared in case. He'd doubled the number of men outside and in. He'd also arranged for the local precinct to do frequent patrols in the neighborhood.

"Wow," Angela said with a laugh, "the NYPD is protecting Anthony Vacarro."

"The Captain and I were in the Marines together," Anthony said, "and besides, it isn't often we have an Assistant Attorney General as a houseguest."

"True, but I'm beginning to think this isn't a lifelong career for me, so think of me as simply Angela, not as Assistant AG."

Chapter 28

Tuesday Morning, May 1, 2012
New York City

The night passed without incident and the next morning as well.

Vincent had a great call with Leonard Shore at 8:30 AM, and the Board meeting that followed was efficient and concise. Vincent was formally elected Acting General Counsel and was given one hundred percent backing from the now shrunken board to oppose the takeover.

"Fighting this takeover is the least we can do for the stockholders and for those that have already given their lives in this sordid mess," Shore said, "but I hear what you are saying, Vincent. It's very possible that with a new Judge, this may all go against us, and time is running very short."

Just before the Board adjournment motion, one of the longest serving Directors said, "You know, Vincent, I've wracked my brain trying to recall any part of our business or operations that could be a hidden treasure. I can't think of anything, but if I were you, I'd look real hard at our real estate. Maybe there's an old gold mine or oil deposit gone dry fifty years ago, and somebody thinks they found a new vein or cache."

"Thanks, Arthur, that's a good suggestion. I don't know exactly how we would find that out, but I'll be on the lookout for anything like that."

Back to Bowdoin College...

Anthony had arranged three different car changes, before they headed to Teterboro, where a Falcon 50 jet was warmed up and waiting for them on the tarmac. He'd arranged for them to fly the private jet to Boston, then change to a second plane, so the flight plans weren't so obvious.

A few hours later, Vincent, Angela and Anthony were in a Suburban on the tarmac of the old Brunswick Naval base, now closed and used for commercial flights. They headed for the Bowdoin College campus, just minutes away.

Vincent and Angela had used the air time to pour over The Sterling Works' records. They each had a flash drive with the financials and notes. They split up the documents. Neither had found anything remotely relevant.

Angela convinced Vincent that he should keep scanning the financials while she dug deeper into the history of Bowdoin's Ghost. Somehow, someway, she felt that if she could unravel the ghost mystery, then it would lead them to a solution.

While Vincent was somewhat convinced by now of The Ghost's existence, he still couldn't see how it could help them with their immediate problem.

"The Ghost isn't going to appear at 10:00 A.M. on Friday morning at Foley Square and argue our case," he'd said.

She conceded the point but was adamant in her position. Probably had something to do with her heritage, he speculated, and frankly, he kind of liked that quality about her.

At 4 PM, Vincent received bad news. Anthony's warning about the Judge swapping was all too accurate. Indeed, Judge Brody had been replaced by a newly-appointed Justice Elizabeth Evoushi who had already advised both counsels to re-brief their positions on disclosure requirements under the 1934 Securities Exchange Act concerning the issue of forcing principals to appear for examination. Oral argument was expected from each side, and it was a clear signal that this new Judge was going to change the ruling. That would mean no disclosure of the real parties in interest and no basis for an injunction. The tender offer could go forward, and then it would all be over.

Vincent was reeling.

But Angela was more determined than ever. "I'm going to dig into the old stacks in Hubbard Hall. Before the new library was built in 1964, Hubbard served as the College's library for many years. It still houses the literature volumes and many historical records."

They split up, agreeing not to break for dinner because time was running out.

Anthony divided his men into two groups. One would watch the entrance to the Hawthorne-Longfellow Building, and the other group went with him to monitor Hubbard.

The hours were burning away. Vincent was in the lower level of Hawthorne. It was now 11 PM, and most of the

Bowdoin students had closed their books for the night. The place was deserted.

Vincent made a brief visit to the rest room. When he returned to his work table, the *Financial Times* was resting on top of his computer. *Strange. It wasn't there before.* He started to toss it aside when his eye caught an article entitled *"China announces 35% reduction on exportation of rare-earth elements, or "REE".*

Vincent paused. REE, what the devil are those, he wondered.

Maybe the reference to China caused him to read the article or perhaps it was simply chance. In any event, he read the piece quickly but thoroughly.

Rare-earth elements were known to a very small section of the general population, but they were 21st Century essentials and becoming more so with each passing day. REEs power virtually all state of the art technology, lasers, microchips, defense systems and so on. The list was endless, and 97% of the world's production of REE was from China. Now, China was reducing the supply to the rest of the world.

Unbelievable, he thought. And then came his enlightenment! Somewhere, deep inside Vincent Mark's brain, there was a major synapse connecting. A real epiphany!

Vincent recalled a detail in the footnotes of one of the old Sterling Works' financials. Something about an option which was listed as an asset but with very little value on the books. It involved land out West.

He started scrolling the documents on his laptop. Ten minutes later, with his heart racing, he found it.

Thirty years ago, in an acquisition of a small manufacturing company, Sterling Works had received an open-ended option on 240,000 acres of land in the North

Fork area of Montana. Never exercised. No reason to exercise it previously. And no expiration on the option. *Is it possible? Could this land have REEs, and the Chinese have discovered that fact? Is that what's behind this monstrous mystery?*

Quickly, he re-Googled REEs and determined that there had recently been a major discovery of REEs deposits north of Montana in Canada, near the border. *This must be it!* He could feel it in his bones. It would explain everything!

He packed up as fast as he could, clutching *The Times'* article. This would not only be unbelievable wealth, perhaps multiple billions, but more importantly, it would mean the way to world domination. The real thing, not the movie version.

He ran out the library door and headed around the corner to Hubbard Hall.

Angela Dominica had lost all track of time. She was way back in Bowdoin's history, reading century-old clips about Pierce, Chamberlain and Peary. She even navigated a website about The Ghost at Bowdoin College, but there was no mention of Jonathan Edwards or his link to any of Bowdoin's famous graduates.

The Hall was eerily silent. All students and staff had long left for their dorms or housing. Angela walked among the stacks, her mind floating high above them.

Then she saw it.

A single, moderately-sized volume with a black leather cover entitled *The Special Records of The Presidents of Bowdoin College, 1806- .* The end year was left blank.

Shaking, she pulled the book from the shelf.

It was all there! Every bit of it. The entire account of Jonathan David Edwards. It recounted the tragic death of his secret fiancée, the three students and their signed confessions, all the incidents of The Ghost at Winthrop Hall, Franklin Pierce, Joshua Chamberlain, Admiral Peary and many more accounts, until 1964.

That's when a lot of new buildings went up, Angela thought, including the new library. Massachusetts Hall, which formerly housed Bowdoin's Presidents, then became the English Department facility. Not long after, a new President came in. The documents and history were thought to be lost. But they've been right here in the Bowdoin stacks all along.

A tsunami of emotions hit Angela. Tears came to her eyes. She wasn't crazy. It all had happened. *My God!*

At that moment, Vincent appeared, gasping for air. "I've got it," he stammered.

Angela hugged him. "And I've found the records of The Ghost, Vincent. It's all true. The Ghost really exists. He's been trying to redeem himself for over two hundred years. He has been trying to help Bowdoin graduates throughout history."

They each poured out the details of their discoveries.

"Obviously, we don't yet have verification that rare-earth elements exist on The Sterling Works' Montana property, but it all fits," Vincent said, still amazed at the information he'd discovered as well as how he discovered it. "This is a story that will blow up everyone connected to it. People in our Government, in Homeland Security, maybe the Secretary himself is conspiring with the Chinese. Treason. Power. Greed and Murder. Cold-blooded Murder. It's all here."

"Yes, it is, but it's too late for both of you."

Vincent and Angela jerked their heads up and turned around to find a tall American with a large Glock, silenced, of course, pointed at them. Their mouths dropped open.

"You've figured it out. Smart bastards! I told our people to take you out right away…Marks and you. An Assistant Attorney General, for God's sake, why did you get mixed up in this? Stupid. And now, you're both dead."

He pointed his weapon directly at Angela.

Vincent stepped in front of her and heard two zips. He looked down at his chest. There was no blood and no pain. He looked up to find the gunman face down with Anthony standing over him.

Anthony kicked away the Glock and checked for a pulse. "He's still alive, but barely."

Vincent and Angela were frozen in place.

The next sixty minutes were a complete blur. Somehow, they all exited Hubbard Hall with Anthony's men assisting. Angela clutched the Presidents' Journal.

The surviving gunman looked like a fellow who'd simply had too much to drink, which is not an uncommon scene at most college campuses, Bowdoin being no exception.

Fortunately, this band of odd fellows narrowly missed Bowdoin's security patrol. The two students who passed them remembered nothing at all about them. They were way too deep in their own thoughts of exams, papers and when they were going to get laid next.

"What made you come into the stacks at that moment?" Angela asked Anthony.

"I followed a white light. I thought it was one of you with a flashlight," he replied. "Did either of you have a flashlight?"

"No," they replied in unison.

"It was The Ghost! He saved our lives, again! I hope this releases him from his guilt," Angela said.

"I don't know, Angela, but I also wonder if it was The Ghost that put *The Times* on my desk."

"I don't know about any ghost," Anthony said, "but it was two real bullets that stopped that bastard from killing you both."

The next forty-eight hours were explosive...

Vincent and the rest of the party left the campus in a hurry. Anthony kept his new prisoner alone and alive for a few hours, although it was touch-and-go. Fortunately, he had the foresight to include one of his Docs in their travel party. Anthony was able to extract all the information the gunman had, which was considerable.

The hearing in New York City on Friday never took place because on Thursday, a front-page story appeared in *The New York Times* and *The Wall Street Journal* exposing the entire Chinese connection, conspiracy and the plot to silently gain control of a cache of rare-earth elements vital for defense systems, located in Montana, which, in turn, was under an obscure, but still valid option to purchase, held by The Sterling Works.

The NYPD and the FBI stormed into action and were all over the homicides and the entire plot. They were no longer restricted by Home Land Security, whose Secretary, quietly resigned for "personal reasons" and then completely disappeared from existence. The second in command at the NSA similarly disappeared, as well as several other high-ranking U.S. officials.

The President did not appear to have any personal involvement and was ignorant of any of these developments, for which he was rightly excoriated, publicly and politically, while Congress fell all over itself in outrage, scheduling hearings and investigations.

The entire affair dominated the news for months as the media ravaged the case.

The Chinese government officially denied any knowledge or involvement in the matter, although eleven prominent Chinese party members and citizens were arrested. Interestingly, they were tried and executed in less than two weeks for unspecified crimes against the Chinese state.

Anthony's wounded assassin was released quietly and without the knowledge of the media or Federal authorities. At the same time, Anthony Vacarro, who had an open IRS investigation pending against him and his businesses, received a personal, handwritten letter from the IRS Commissioner stating that all inquiries were now concluded and satisfactorily resolved with no penalties.

Leonard Shore recovered from his wounds and returned to the Board of The Sterling Works, which suddenly found itself atop a multi-billion-dollar asset. Their stock soared.

Vincent Mark was made Senior Vice President and General Counsel and was elected to the Board. He also received a five-million-dollar net cash bonus along with hefty awards of Sterling Works stock and options.

Angela Dominica resigned her position with the New York Attorney General's office, disillusioned with her boss and the entire system. However, the Attorney General did make sure to return from Bermuda in time to have the New York Legislature pass a Special Resolution of Commendation for her along with a large, wooden plaque embossing the same. She wasn't unemployed for more than twenty-four hours before accepting a partnership in a high-profile Criminal Defense firm, which occasionally, handled matters for one Anthony Vacarro and his Associates. She also signed a lucrative contract with S. Holmes Publishing that came with a $500,000 advance. The book was to be entitled *The Ghost of Bowdoin College*. Angela donated $250,000 of her advance to the Bowdoin College Scholarship Fund, in memory of Jonathan David Edwards.

Anthony Vacarro's legend and reputation grew even stronger and more widespread, given the failure of a Swiss mercenary commando unit to destroy his compound and kill him along with his family and Vincent and Angela. His wife continued to make homemade ravioli and marinara sauce for dinner every Monday night, which was faithfully attended by Vincent Mark.

Vincent kept his date with Sofia and continued to see her frequently, but he also occasionally had dinner or caught a show with Angela.

Late Fall 2012, in State Supreme Court, Vincent Mark appeared before Judge Robert X. Tucci. Vincent had made peace with himself and his past. He knew who he was and who he wasn't. The application before the Court was to change his name back to Vincent Marcantonio. It was approved without comment by the Court.

And finally...

What, you may wonder, became of The Ghost?

Was the apparition just a lot of silly nonsense?

Hardly, my friends, for this entire story is true, and I, The Ghost of Bowdoin College, have faithfully relayed it to you as accurately as is possible.

But, then again, ghosts don't exist, right?

THE END... *maybe*

About the Author

Giuseppe Vincenzo Vumbacco is the Italian version of my American name. I hold degrees from Bowdoin College (1967 - English); Syracuse University College of Law, cum laude, 1970; and, a Certification of Completion of Finance for Senior Executives from the Harvard Business School. In the early 1970's, I practiced corporate law with Mudge Rose Guthrie & Alexander in Manhattan, then went on to hold senior executive positions with two NYSE firms. In 2001, I became Chief Executive Officer and President of then HMA (NYSE), a Fortune 600 Company from which I retired at age 62. I then engaged a private tutor to learn Italian because I didn't want to die speaking only English. I have also served on a number of public, private and non-profit Boards of Directors. I am a 32nd degree Master Mason and one of the founders of Jubilee Fellowship of Naples, a non-denominational Christian Church in Naples, Florida. My wife and I have been married for more than 52 years, have two adult children and five grandchildren (the eldest of whom is enrolled at Bowdoin), and we divide our time among Florida, New York and Maine.

Books by the Author

<u>Money. Murder. And the Mob.</u>:

The Ghost of Bowdoin College

The Bowdoin Ghost Returns --- *Coming soon!*

Note from The Author:

Dear Reader,
I hope you enjoyed The Ghost of Bowdoin College. It was a
long journey (of ten years) writing this story, but a
satisfying personal experience. The next book in this series
will be "The Bowdoin Ghost Returns", and it will begin
with the story of Anthony Vacarro. It should be available in
six to eight months, not ten years. If you want to contact
me, email me at joe@giuseppevumbacco.com. Thank you
for your support ---
Giuseppe Vincenzo Vumbacco

Made in the USA
Columbia, SC
07 February 2019